TIM MENDEES

A NOVELLA

MIRACLE GROWTH

MIRACLE GROWTH

A NOVELLA

BY TIM MENDEES

EERIE RIVER PUBLISHING
www.EerieRiverPublishing.com

Eerie River Publishing
www.EerieRiverPublishing.com
Hamilton, Ontario Canada

Paperback ISBN: 978-1-990245-53-4
Digital ISBN: 978-1-990245-52-7

Edited by S.O. Green & Michelle River
Cover Art by Michelle River

ALSO BY TIM MENDEES

THE HOLLOWHILLS CYCLE:

Burning Reflection (2020)
Boiling Shadow (2021)

SHORT STORY COLLECTION:

The Pseudopod That Rocks The Cradle (2021)

NOVELLAS:

Spiffing (2021)
The Creeping Void (2021)
The Grime of the Ancient Mariner (2021)

EERIE ANTHOLOGIES:

It Calls From the Forest (2020)
It Calls From the Sky (2020)
It Calls From the Sea (2021)
Midnight Shadows (2021)
After (2021)
Monsters and Mayhem (2022)

For Linda, H.P. Lovecraft and John Wyndham.

INTRODUCTION

Exhaling a cloud of pungent smoke, Johnny Green reclined in the deckchair he had recently liberated from the nearby pier. The colourful, striped fabric stood out in stark contrast to the harsh, breeze block walls of the converted garage. Across from him, another man sat on an overturned beer crate, grinning inanely and cutting the bottom off an old plastic milk bottle with a pair of rusty tin snips.

"Ruddy hell," Johnny croaked, desperately trying not to choke. "This stuff ain't 'alf got a kick to it."

Pete Prince looked up, his vision taking seconds to catch up with his eyeballs. "Aye. You just wait until we get this bucket bong up an' running. Have ye put a hole in that lid yet?"

Johnny put the cardboard roach of his expertly rolled spliff to his cracked lips and inhaled, holding it for a few seconds before billowing smoke out of his nostrils. "Look, I'm a dragon." He giggled, passing Pete the blue plastic lid with a rough, circular hole gouged in the centre.

"Yer a daft twat." Pete rolled his eyes and took the lid from his friend's trembling fingers. "Make yerself useful for a change. Go an' get the bucket ready."

"Aye, alright. Here, hold this for a second." Johnny passed Pete the pungent reefer and prepared for the herculean task of extracting his flabby rump from the sagging deckchair. The wooden frame creaked and groaned as he waddled it from side to side, struggling to sit forward.

Pete put the spliff in his mouth and took a drag. "Need a hand?" Pete put the spliff in his mouth and took a drag.

"Nah, I got it. Just gimme a minute... Right, here we go!" With a groan of exertion, Johnny shot forwards and landed on all fours on a tatty sheepskin rug. Pete nearly choked. Smoke and laughter burst from his lungs in heaving gusts.

"Piss off," Johnny giggled, using the deckchair to pull himself to his feet. "It's this weed, man. It's knocked me sideways. My legs feel like a couple of jelly worms."

"I used to love those... Now, stop arsing about an' get some water the bucket. We're almost ready to rock and roll."

"Alright, alright. Hold yer horses, stroppy bollocks." Johnny swayed, eyes drifting around their clubhouse. It was a large double garage set back from the nearby housing estate. Shadows cast by two standing lamps danced as whorls of light from a collection of lava lamps and a purring bubble tube spread across the walls. The bucket was over by the bar.

Squeezing between the end of their rickety pool table and one of the sliding garage doors, Johnny made his way unsteadily over. The bar was their pride and joy. The two layabouts had cobbled it together from the remains of a wardrobe they'd fished from a skip and other scavenged household detritus. Unfortunately, both men had played hooky on the day their woodwork teacher taught the rest of the class how to use a spirit level. The top of the bar was as crooked as a dog's hind leg.

Being careful not to trip over the extension cord that ran to their greenhouse, he picked up the bucket, turned, and looked at the plastic sheeting separating the back third of the room. "You know, Pete? I feel a little bit like Adam."

"What, him that works at the Post Office?"

"Nah, you twonk. *The* Adam. You know, him from the Bible."

"Ah. Gotcha." Pete snipped off the last of the milk carton's rough plastic edges and frowned. "Eh? Why's that? I 'ope you ain't calling me Eve."

"Behold!" He spread his arms towards the plastic sheets covered in condensation and lit by UV lights. "Our garden of Eden."

At this, Pete smiled and nodded. "Nice. Though, if either of us is Adam, it's me. It was my idea, and you're the one with the cleavage, so..."

Johnny flipped Pete a V then carried on with his task. "Seriously, I've got to hand it to you Pete, me old fruit. That was a stroke of genius." He pointed to the greenhouse, then waddled past his compatriot, tapping along to the Bob Marley song coming from their tinny hi-fi speakers on the edge of the metal pail. "We should set up another one on my mum's allotment. She hardly uses it these days...and she wouldn't know a marijuana plant if it bit her on the backside. In six months, we'd be loaded!"

Before Pete could reply, there was a rustle from behind

the sheet. "Shh, you hear that?"

Johnny cocked his head like a puppy, as if that would help his auditory prowess. "Nope. What?"

"There was a rustling noise, off in the corner."

"Probably a field mouse. Little buggers are always at my mum's herbs."

Pete shrugged and took another toke.

Rustle...

"There," Pete spluttered, "you hear it this time?"

"Yeah, I still reckon it's a mouse."

"Bloody big mouse," Pete said flatly. "Sounded more like a rat."

Johnny froze. "Don't say that, dude... I fuckin' hate rats."

"Don't be such a pussy. It'll probably leg it when you go in there. Anyway, one nibble of that lot an' it'll be on its back with its legs in the air singing Elvis songs. Just scoop it into the bucket and dump it outside."

"What if it ain't?" Johnny was being inexorably dragged into the paranoia part of the stoner experience. His voice had taken on a whiny, nasal tone, like a schoolboy that had been denied sweets by a parent.

"Then," Pete looked around and picked up the mallet he used to break up lumps of cannabis resin, "wallop it on the head with this." He grinned and tossed the camping implement at his friend.

Johnny tried to catch it, but he was too fried. It clattered to the floor between his legs, narrowly missing his sandaled feet. He looked down at it for a few seconds before shaking his head and putting the bucket down. "Nah. Bollocks to this. I'm not having a punch up with a bloody rat. I've seen the size of the buggers around here. Big as a Jack Russell terrier some of 'em. They go for your throat if you corner 'em. A mate of mine that works down the Caxton said one jumped over his shoulder when he took the bins out one night. Bloody agile little buggers, they are. Plus, their piss is infectious!"

"For fuck's sake, Johnny. Get a grip."

"Nah. Screw it. I don't want Weil's disease, bubonic plague, or some other nasty shit. If you're so brave, you do it."

Pete held a lungful of smoke for a few seconds and absent-mindedly scratched at the track marks on his emaciated arms. Finally, he released it, blowing fat rings that drifted slowly towards the ceiling. "Fine. I'll do it. Anything to stop you whining."

Rustle...

Johnny yelped and leapt away from their marijuana garden, nearly colliding with Pete as he unsteadily got to his feet.

"Watch it, you big lummox." Pete had to put his hand on the cold metal door to steady himself. Once his legs had decided to work, he shuffled over to Johnny, who was staring intently through the sheeting, looking for movement. Pete nudged him with his elbow, making him yelp a second time. "Pass me the bucket."

"Here," Johnny did as he was told for a change. "You'd better take this as well," he thrust the mallet into Pete's hands.

Pete took the weapon and ambled towards the end of

the curtain. "Right, I'm going in. If I don't come back within the hour..." He paused for dramatic effect. "Send a search party."

"You're such a twat." Johnny giggled despite himself. Damn, their homegrown weed was strong. "Just be careful, dude."

"Alright, mum. Will do." Using the mallet's handle, Pete pulled the curtain aside and stepped gingerly over the head of the extension cord. It was an electrician's nightmare. The four sockets were stacked with multi-plugs like some bizarre form of Tetris. Cables ran in all directions, feeding the UV lights that hung haphazardly from nails and rolls of gaffer tape. More plugs fed their rudimentary hydroponics setup made from cannibalised aquarium pumps and lengths of plastic hosepipe. It was a wonder the garage hadn't burst into flames.

"Can you see it?"

Pete peered into the depths of their illegal jungle. "Nah," he shrugged, letting the curtain fall behind him. "It must have gone."

Johnny breathed a sigh of relief. "Cool. I'll get another spliff on the go." As he plonked himself down on the beer crate and placed the tea tray containing their rolling paraphernalia on his lap, there was a series of loud rustles from behind the curtain.

"What the fu—?" Pete trailed off. His voice was muffled by the purr of the water pumps.

Johnny looked over, "What is it?"

"I dunno. It's...ack!" Pete started to make choking noises as the plants rustled like crazy. The bucket hit the concrete with a clang, making Johnny jump out of his skin.

Johnny leapt to his feet, overturning the tray and showering their collection of rugs with crumpled rolling papers and bits of torn cardboard. "Pete, you alright, dude?"

The rustling stopped, and all was quiet.

"Pete?" Johnny started to edge towards the curtain. "Come on, dude. Stop arsing around." As he got closer, he could hear a strange gurgling sound. He smiled to himself. "Very funny. The rat got you by the throat, has it?"

The gurgling stopped, and there was a sharp thump against the wall. The smile fell from Johnny's lips. "Come on, man. Cut it out. This is about as funny as a dose of the clap!"

Something brushed against the plastic sheet, making Johnny flinch. His heart was hammering, throat constricting, head spinning. "Pete? You alright back there?"

When nothing happened for a few moments, his mind began to race. *What if he's had an allergic reaction? What if he electrocuted himself? What if the rat is eating his face? What if there are hundreds of rats?*

Screwing his fists tight, he tried to get a grip. "Stop it, you silly bugger. He's just trying to freak you out."

Steeling himself, Johnny snatched the curtain and pulled it back...

"Ha. Ha. Very funny. Okay, you got me..."

He gasped.

"Holy shi—"

The plants started to rustle.

Johnny screamed.

CHAPTER 1

The annual flower show at the Betyls Cove summer fete was something of a cut-throat affair. Admittedly, nobody had ever actually had their throats cut, though it had degenerated into pruning shears at dawn on several occasions. Contestants had been known to sabotage soil, introduce pests, and even stoop to straight-up flower assassination. Nothing chilled a gardener's soul like a row of decapitated begonias. But, as competitive as the flower show could be, it paled in comparison to the vegetable competition.

While the flower show was mainly the domain of the local Women's Institute, the vegetable growing contest was dominated by red-faced men in tweed. As was to be expected, testosterone and competitive pride turned the post-competition pub session into an out-and-out bloodbath, as farmers and amateurs alike scuffled over prize rosettes. Pubs in the area had been known to hire bouncers for the weekend.

Some of those proud local soil tenders would try anything to get an advantage, from commercially purchased fertilizers to home-spun tonics passed down from generation to generation. Some would use all manner of weird and wonderful concoctions; not quite 'ear of bat' and 'eye of newt', but some of them could get a little outré.

On the other side of the fence, more scrupulous growers refused to lower themselves to such things, preferring an organic approach. Trickier to pull off, but it often reaped the best results.

Jim Matthews was one such man. He'd been growing prize marrows since he was a young lad, under the supervision of his father and grandfather. Both patriarchs were prize-winning growers in their own right, and Jim was honoured to carry on the noble tradition.

Jim prided himself that he didn't have to resort to underhand tactics or bizarre potions to grow a decent marrow. He'd been winning his category since he'd retired. When it came to rearing marvellous marrows, Jim was unstoppable. Unfortunately, this year was proving to be something of a nightmare.

"Blast it!" Jim plonked his handled glass on the pub table and glared at his cards. "I'm out... Story of my life at the minute." He tossed his cards onto the table and pouted. That was three hands in a row he'd been cleaned out. If he hadn't been the dealer of the last hand, he'd have been convinced it was rigged.

The man opposite him, a grizzled pensioner called Geoff Davis, peered over his own hand, bushy eyebrows knitting together, and fixed Jim with a stare. "What's up with you tonight, Jim? You've had a face like a smacked arse ever since you turned up."

"Oh..." Jim exhaled, puckering his lips and shaking his head. "It's my marrow..."

"Go and see a doctor." Tony, the third occupant of the corner table of the Ancient Mariner public house, grinned as he tossed a couple of copper coins into the growing pot.

"Very funny." Jim glared at his old schoolmate. "You know what I mean. I'm having no luck with 'em this year."

"What's the problem?" Geoff asked. He too, was a grower, though he stuck to carrots and parsnips, and was nowhere near Jim's level of expertise.

"You know last year, we had that marvellous spring? Well, I took my marrows out of the poly-tunnel early and hit the jackpot. They turned out ruddy marvellous. Some of the best marrows I've ever grown."

"Aye, that was a good year. Unseasonably warm it was." Geoff nodded. "You should have seen the size of me carrots."

Tony sniggered. The others rolled their eyes. It was the same every Saturday when they met up for their weekly libation. Tony would have a few, and before you knew it, it was like sitting in the pub with Benny Hill. Everything was an innuendo or filthy euphemism.

"Well, when we had that glorious few weeks in April, I..."

"You didn't!" Geoff cut in. "You didn't gamble on the weather?"

Jim nodded solemnly.

"Oh, rookie mistake," Tony piped up. "Gambling on the weather in Cornwall is about as sensible as playing Russian roulette with six loaded chambers. Every grower worth his salt knows that. You can get all four seasons in a day around here."

"I know, I know..." Jim pinched the bridge of his bulbous nose. "I've just been feeling the pressure from 'im down the road. He nearly beat me last year, and I wanted to get a head start. Then, we had that frost..."

Geoff slurped the last of his pint. "Aye, bitter it was." Geoff slurped the last of his pint.

"Bitter? It was like the hand of death creeping over my allotment. I lost some of my best specimens. The others..." He held his hands about twelve inches apart. "I nearly cried when I got my tape measure out.

Tony was preparing to make a smutty remark but stopped himself. Poor Jim looked like he was about to burst into tears there and then. Instead, he finished his jar and placed it next to Geoff's. "Whose round is it?"

"Jim's."

Jim sighed. "Of course it is. Fine, same again?"

Geoff and Tony nodded.

As Jim drained his dregs and rose, Tony had a brainwave. "Why don't you go an' 'ave a chat with Big Mick at the bar?" He gestured towards a man that looked akin to an orange grizzly bear encased in tweed.

"Oh, you know me, Tone. I don't go in for any of the weird stuff he pedals."

Big Mick was something of a character on the vegetable circuit. He was the fixer, the man who could get you whatever you wanted, whenever you wanted it. Mick had so many fingers in so many pies he'd had to start using his toes and other, less sanitary, appendages. If you wanted horse manure from derby winning thoroughbreds, or ancient soil from a church sepulchre, then Big Mick was your man. However, his main export was growth hormones and things of that nature. The stronger and more illegal, the better.

"It ain't just chemical stuff he's got," Tony insisted.

"Yeah, I don't believe any of that gumpf about 'hallowed soil' he spouts to the old dears down the bingo. It's all a big con."

"Nah, I ain't on about that stuff. My Alice told me about a friend of hers that goes to the WI meetings, Patty something-or-other. She grows Dahlias for the show and was 'aving a similar problem to you. Anyway, she bought this new kind of compost off Mick and Bob's-your-uncle. Looks like she's set to win again. Says the blooms are as big as ruddy dinner plates."

"Really? And, there's nothing funny about the stuff? He's not laced it with steroids or some madness?"

"Nah. Old Patty's just as barmy as you." Tony grinned, exposing the gap in his front teeth. "She won't even *eat* anything that ain't one hundred per cent organic, never mind put her precious dahlias in chemicals. I don't get it myself. A carrot's a bloody carrot, at the end of the day. Who cares where it came from?"

Jim looked at his friend, aghast at the heresy he'd just spewed.

Geoff cut in before Jim could let rip. His friend had a tendency to become a tad evangelical about vegetables, and he liked to avoid a sermon wherever possible. "This stuff.

'ow much is he chargin' for it? I might have to get me a bag or two."

Jim winced as he straightened his back and collected the glasses. Turning away, he left Tony telling Geoff how much Patty had spent and wondered how she could afford it. This inevitably led him to moan about his paltry state pension, a conversation that Jim was only too glad to escape. Weaving through the tables and ducking under the old oak beams decorated with fishing memorabilia, he made his way slowly to the bar and his potential saviour, Mick Bradshaw. Sidling along the bar, he clunked the glasses down next to Mick and gave him a nod of greeting. "Alright, Mick. How's it going?"

Mick loved his cider, and had obviously been loving it passionately for most of the afternoon. His cheeks were glowing rosy red, and a wide, boozy grin was plastered across his bewhiskered jowls. "Art'noon, Jim. It's all good. Business is boomin'," he slurred. "'ow's the marrows?"

Jim removed his flat cap and rubbed his thinning head of silver hair. "Ah, not good, Mick. That frost last month did for most of 'em." Jim removed his flat cap and rubbed his thinning head of silver hair.

"Sorry to 'ear that."

"I haven't a blasted hope of holding on to my title at this rate." He sighed. "I might even be forced to forfeit." The word sent a shudder down the old man's spine. It was unthinkable that a Matthews would suffer such an ignoble blow.

Mick scratched his ginger whiskers and spoke in a low

voice. "I might 'ave a little somethin' that could change your fortune, me old mucker."

"Yeah, Tony said you might be able to help."

"That, I may…" Mick's demeanour was conspiratorial. He cast furtive glances around the crowded bar to ensure no ears were flapping. "I got 'old of this new compost, see?"

"Oh, aye?" Jim did his best to hide his scepticism.

"It's a new product, made right 'ere in the Cove," Mick continued, his breath like paint stripper. "It ain't on the market yet, so it's a bit 'ush-'ush, but it works bloody wonders. Me missus put some under 'er tomatoes, and you should see the size of the ruddy things!" His eyes lit up, and balls of saliva started to grow in the corners of his mouth. "Taste amazin' an' all, they do."

"Really?" Jim was starting to feel warm, fuzzy flushes of optimism. "What's in it then?"

"Don't rightly know. I 'eard that it comes from the cave under the Blasted Crag. Ye know, where the meteor struck back in the day?"

"Oh, aye?" Jim cocked an eyebrow, optimism on the wane again.

"They reckon the soil in the caves is imbued with some minerals or summat from the meteor that makes stuff grow quick. I 'ave a few bags in the back of me Land Rover. I can sell you some if you want it?"

Jim struggled internally for a couple of moments. Using miracle formulas to aid growth went against all of his principles. He looked upon those who resorted to such things as mere amateurs, dabblers in the green-fingered arts, but he was in a right old fix. His back was against the shed wall. And it wasn't like it was against the rules or anything.

Finally, Jim made his decision. "What the hell... It can't make my chances of winning any worse. Even if it poisons the buggers, it can't put me in a worse state than I'm in now. How much do you want for it?" He reached into his pocket and retrieved his battered leather wallet.

Mick grinned before walloping back the remaining third of his pint in one hearty gulp. "How many ye want? I do discounts fer bulk orders." Mick grinned before walloping back the remaining third of his pint in one hearty gulp.

"Just the one, for now, Mick. I want to see how it goes."

"Cautious as ever, I see." Mick leaned in so close his beard was tickling Jim's cheek. "Tell ye what. I can do you a big bag for ten quid…and a refill." He rattled his empty glass on the bar, attracting the attention of the barmaid.

"Go on then," Jim said, whipping out a tenner. "You've got yourself a deal."

"Proper job!" Mick chuckled and snatched the note from Jim's fingers, rolling it and slipping it into his inside pocket. "You get the drinks in, an' I'll go fetch it." Slapping Jim on the shoulder with enough force it was a wonder he didn't dislocate it, Mick hopped off his stool and weaved towards the door. As he went, he started to belt out a dirty sea shanty at extreme volume. Jim shook his head and began to question whether he'd have been better off buying magic beans.

"Righto, what can I get yer?" a husky female voice asked, snapping Jim out of his funk.

"Oh, erm… Two pints of IPA, one pint of best, and whatever rocket fuel Mick is on, please, Martha."

"Right you are."

As Martha Green busied herself pulling pints of ale, Jim stood and pondered his decision. In the end, optimism won out. If Mick's compost was as good as he said it was, he would romp home with first place easily. He started to smile. Things were finally looking up. When he returned to the table and distributed the drinks, Jim was back to his usual chipper self.

"Sorted?" Geoff asked.

Jim nodded. "Sorted." Jim nodded.

"Well," Tony said, raising his glass, "Here's to Jim's marvellous marrows!"

Jim beamed and took a gulp. This pint tasted better than the previous two. Evidently, they had changed the barrel at last. It looked like his luck was finally changing for the better. And who said no good ever came from buying things from strange men in pubs?

CHAPTER 2

Buttered crumpets, three rashers of streaky bacon, two butcher's sausages, and a poached egg was Jim's patented hangover cure. Without fail, it settled the stomach and cleared the head. After this reinvigorating repast and two cups of hot, sweet tea, he was ready to face the day. Truth be told, he'd bounced out of bed that morning, which was something of a minor miracle, as he'd drunk more the previous evening than a man of his age should. The thought of Mick's compost had him feeling like a kid on Christmas morning.

His wife had gone out early to take care of some WI business over at the church—the head of the guild, Ivy Finch, had decided that the rectory was getting a good clean, whether the vicar liked it or not—leaving Jim free to potter.. Once his breakfast had settled, he was ready to trudge on over to the allotment and give the wonder compost a try. Clad in his favourite green wellies and his best flat cap, Jim stepped out into the daylight.

It was a clear, fresh morning, alive with joyful birdsong, as Jim arrived at his allotment. Betyls Cove council had turned several acres of disused MOD land behind the Edwards Estate over to the local populace for growing purposes. Jim had been lucky enough to snag a modest plot before the waiting list had grown to ridiculous proportions. Hefting the fifty-litre bag out of his Volvo, he slung it over his bony shoulder and walked the hundred yards to his shed, then placed it next to his wheelbarrow.

The bag was a nondescript, vacuum-packed bundle made from bin-liner plastic. Its only distinguishing feature was a sticky label with the word 'Compost' scrawled on it with a felt pen. Using a pair of secateurs, Jim carefully slit it open.

"Cor, blimey!" Jim recoiled, gagging as the pungent stench of decay and seawater assailed his nostrils. "Stinks like a merman's lavatory. "He snatched his handkerchief out of his green body warmer and clamped it over his mouth. Once the breeze had gotten rid of the worst of the noxious odour, he tipped the compost into his rickety, old wheelbarrow and left it to breathe. Thankful his marrows weren't downwind of the reeking compost, he set about carefully digging out his crop. They were still woefully under par.

"There you go, my little beauties," he said in a tender voice, once they had all been exhumed. "Time to get you in some nice, new compost. It'll make you big and strong." He always spoke to his marrows that way. It was one of the main bones of contention between him and his wife. If he talked to her the same way he did to them every now and again, their marriage would be infinitely more harmonious.

Holding his breath, Jim replaced the earth around them with his new miracle compost. After his babies were comfortably rebedded, he poured himself a nice cup of tea from his Thermos. Reclined in his deckchair, he prayed to whatever department of Heaven dealt with vegetables that Mick's quick fix would work. "If this doesn't work...I'm sunk."

Jim awoke the following morning feeling bright and breezy. He showered, headed downstairs and prepared breakfast. As he skimmed the local paper looking for anything vaguely interesting, his wife, Marjorie, appeared in the doorway in her postal uniform. She marched over to the breakfast table and scooped up one half of her bacon sandwich.

"What are you going to do with yourself today? Sit on your idle backside in front of the telly, I presume?" Marjorie had a face like thunder and a tongue like lightning. She was moody at the best of times, but she hadn't slept well and that never boded well.

Jim opened his mouth to protest but thought better of it. Instead, he dabbed at a blob of brown sauce with the crust of his sandwich.

"I can't wait to retire," Marjorie continued, swallowing a mouthful of fried pig. "Then we can both lounge around without a bloody care in the world."

Again, Jim stayed silent. As she threw on her blue jacket and peaked cap, he had to stifle a chuckle. She always reminded him of a bad-tempered version of Mrs Goggins from Postman Pat when she was in one of her moods.

"I bet you're off down the allotment."

"Yeah, I..."

"Maybe you'd pay me more attention if I had roots."

"Look, I…"

"Just make sure you do the washing up. I always have to do everything around here."

"Yes, dear."

"And, take the bins out."

"Yes, dear."

"And, run the hoover 'round."

"Yes, dear."

"Right, I'm off." Marjorie gave Jim a perfunctory peck on the cheek, stuffed the remnants of her sandwich into her face, then left.

Jim sighed in relief and returned his attention to the newspaper. After a while, he folded it up and shoved it over to his wife's side of the table. Following a final, satisfying gulp of tea, he got up and did the dishes at warp speed. The vacuuming could wait until later. He had far more pressing matters to attend to.

With his trusty tape measure in his pocket and a flask of tea, he took a leisurely stroll down to the allotment. It was surprisingly busy. Almost every plot was a hive of activity. It was the same every year in the run-up to the show, but this was above and beyond. He'd never seen so many people on the allotments at one time. Without giving it much thought, he scuttled to his shed, put his flask next to his stained metal cup, and tuned his radio to Classic FM.

With anticipation tingling in his fingertips, he retrieved a spade and dug up one of his marrows. He couldn't believe his eyes when he held the tape measure against the striped cultivar. It appeared to have grown an inch and a half overnight. If his legs hadn't been riddled with arthritis, he would have danced a jig around his shed. He was so happy that he celebrated by putting a tot of brandy from the half-bottle hidden under a mountain of seed packets into his tea.

So began the most exciting week in Jim's life since his honeymoon.

On inspection the following day, the rate of growth was the same. And it was the same the next day and the next. It appeared the miraculous compost was prompting his marrows to grow three inches every two days. Jim couldn't believe his luck. After all that stress and worry, it really looked like he was in with a shot of keeping his crown.

When Friday rolled around again, Jim set out for his weekly night out down the pub with Geoff and Tony. Despite usually paying for everything on his debit card, Jim made a detour via a cash machine and withdrew twenty pounds. Jim fully intended to show Mick his gratitude for yanking him out of the hole by lining his pocket and filling his capacious belly with cider. By now, he was the proud owner of the largest marrows he had ever seen and was a dead cert for the gold rosette.

Jim's spirits were high as he sank his first of several pints of best bitter. "Pub's quiet tonight," he mused aloud.

"Aye," Geoff nodded. "It's been goin' downhill since the new landlord took over."

Jim looked around. While it was true the crowd was

slowly shrinking, he'd never seen it this quiet. It was like the Mary Celeste.

"Frank's on about closin' for a bit and reopening as a gastropub," Tony whispered. The landlord, Frank, was currently behind the bar and not a man to cross.

"That'll never work. Frank couldn't cook a decent bit of grub if his life depended on it," Geoff wheezed. He looked terrible. His skin was waxy, and his eyes bloodshot.

"You feelin' alright, mate?" Tony asked.

"Yeah, you look like hell," Jim agreed.

"Cheers, Jim. I love you too." Geoff managed a weak smile. "Aye, I'm alright. My IBS is playing up, is all. I was up all night on the bog. My guts feel like a washing machine."

"Too much information." Tony grimaced theatrically before changing the subject. "Anyway, Jim. How goes the marrows?"

"Bloody brilliant! Mick's compost worked a treat. That stuff's a Godsend. Did you get any in the end, Geoff?"

"Aye, I bought a bag when I saw him at market last Saturday. My parsnips are comin' along nicely. I might even get onto the podium this year. We 'ad some of the carrots yesterday with dinner. Beautiful, they were. I dunno if it's something to do with the sea salt, but they hardly needed seasoning. Best carrots I've ever tasted."

Jim watched as beads of saliva formed in the corners of his friend's mouth. It reminded him of Mick's reaction when he spoke of his wife's tomatoes. This made him look over to Mick's perch, but he wasn't there. Just an empty barstool. This was odd. Big Mick practically lived in the pub.

"Was Mick in before I arrived?"

"Nah." Tony shrugged. "I ain't seen him since Wednesday. Although, I've hardly been out. The missus has got me decorating again."

"Geoff?"

"Eh? Oh, sorry... Miles away. What's the question?"

"Have you seen Mick today?"

Geoff thought for a minute, rubbing his glassy eyes. "Today, nope. He's probably having a couple 'round the Caxton. Flogging some more compost, no doubt. You know Mick; he'll be along later. Never misses a Friday, does Mick."

All three heads turned in anticipation as the door opened. For a second, Jim's heart soared...then sank. It wasn't Mick. It was a little old lady clutching a ten-pound note in her wizened fingers. Peering out from beneath her crotchet bobble hat, she scanned the bar. Upon seeing Mick's empty stool, her shoulders sagged. Deflated, she hurried from the pub.

"That's the fourth one so far," Tony said, emptying his glass.

"Eh?"

"Beryl Wingate, she was holding a tenner. Must be looking for Mick. After some more compost, no doubt. Why else would a teetotaller come into the Mariner on a Friday night? There's been three other people come in an' do the exact same thing. Come in, look forlornly at Mick's stool, then bugger off."

Jim finished his drink. "It's my round, ain't it?" he asked, collecting up the empties.

Geoff and Tony nodded. Jim couldn't help but smile. They looked like the plastic dogs you saw in the back windows of family estate cars. Navigating the empty stools, he approached the bar, put the glasses down and nodded at the behemoth next to the pumps. "Same again, please, Frank."

Frank grunted, which was an improvement on usual. He was a taciturn chap, built like a brick outhouse, with no neck, bulging eyes, and a wide, frog-like mouth. If beauty was only skin deep, then ugliness went right to the bone. His personality was just as unpleasant. A great white shark would have had better people skills than Frank…No wonder the pub was failing.

"Hey, Frank. Has Mick been in?"

"Nah." Frank paused in his task and grinned. Jim nearly had a heart attack; he'd never seen Frank smile before and it was unsettling, to say the least. His teeth were pointy and jagged, and there looked to be hundreds of them. "I 'eard 'ee's ill. 'ad a dodgy pie 'round the Caxton. That'll teach the bugger. That's what you get for eatin' their muck. You wait 'til we go gastro. I'll show 'em what pub grub should taste like."

Pub landlords could be bitchy, but Frank put the average fashion model to shame.

Jim forced a smile as Frank continued to chuckle. After all, what was funnier than one of your customers lying ill in bed with food poisoning?

"Here ye go. Two IPA, one best."

Frank put the pints down on a tray in front of Jim and held out the card reader.

Jim hovered his debit card over the screen, there was a sharp beep, and he was away. After placing the drinks on the table in front of their rightful owners, Jim sat down with a thump.

"No sign of Mick?" Tony inquired, supping the froth of his golden pint.

Jim shook his head. "Frank reckons he's got bad guts from a dodgy pie."

"Poor sod," Geoff winced, clearly in discomfort. "Speaking of bad guts, excuse me, lads." With that, he bolted from the table in the direction of the gents. As Jim watched the door slam behind his friend, he couldn't help but feel a pang of unease. Geoff didn't look well. Maybe Mick didn't have food poisoning at all. Maybe there was a stomach bug going around.

Not wanting to dwell on the subject, he took a swig of beer and gazed out of the window into the yard.

Tony nudged Jim with his elbow and nodded to the door. "Here's another one, look." Another dejected pensioner was looking around, holding her purse. It was becoming obvious that Jim wasn't the only one missing Mick that night. An impromptu gathering of the town's green-fingered growers seemed to be occurring. As the night wore on, a seemingly never-ending stream of entrants for the flower and vegetable shows appeared in the doorway, ten-pound notes in their grubby fingers. One by one, they left, sullen, downbeat, and dejected.

Jim gulped as realisation dawned. Mick's miracle compost had been making many gardeners very happy, but now the supply had been cut off. It was akin to when the local drug dealer was on holiday at Her Majesty's pleasure. The realisation blossomed into a big, black flower of pessimism. If everyone was using the same stuff, he still hadn't a hope in hell of winning.

The rest of the evening's drinks tasted somewhat sour...

CHAPTER 3

Two days before the show, Jim had yet another blazing row with his wife. It was one of those pointless rows that married couples have about curtains or fabric softener, nothing of any consequence or importance. Whenever this happened, Jim would skulk off down the allotment to sulk while his wife simmered down. He waited until she had gone upstairs, filled his flask, and left via the back door.

It was early evening by the time Jim reached his sanctuary, so he tuned in to Radio Four, poured himself a cup of tea and settled down with his newspaper. It was a balmy night, with a slight breeze rustling the branches of the enclosing trees. They swayed along to the soothing music from the wireless. As he reclined in his chair, his eyelids began to sag. Before you could say 'gardener's question time', Jim was drifting off into the arms of Morpheus.

Jim dreamed of his own personal Eden. A wondrous place, filled with six-foot marrows and pumpkins so large you could live inside them. He wandered around, tending to his plants together with his Eve—Marjorie, the way she'd been before their marriage soured. He was content, and would have stayed there longer, had a furtive rustle not woken him with a start.

"Eh?" Jim sat up, bewildered. The curtains of slumber hadn't fully parted, so for a second, he thought the scene before him was some kind of fever dream. Night had fallen and thick tendrils of mist swirled around the allotment, licking the vegetation and coiling around the bamboo canes. Jim shook his head to clear the cobwebs. What he was seeing boggled the mind. The allotment was lit by an unearthly glow. It couldn't possibly be real... Could it?

"What the hell?" he muttered, as he looked around. Aside from a rectangle of dim, yellow light spreading from his open shed door, there was no other source of illumination. "Where the bloody hell is that coming from?"

Jim stood and wandered to what appeared to be the source of the glow.

"What in God's name?"

An unearthly light radiated from the patch of earth around his precious marrows. If he had been pressed to identify a single colour, he'd have failed. Before his mind could register what his eyes were seeing, it shifted into something new and unfathomable. It was like nothing he'd ever seen before.

Crouching cautiously to get a better look, he caught a whiff of something ghastly. Gagging and spluttering, he covered his mouth with his hand. The already foul aroma of Mick's compost had mingled with something sickly sweet. He couldn't bear it for more than a few seconds so he returned to his upright posture and looked around. By now, the mist was hanging over his plot like a shroud.

"This ain't natural," he muttered to himself. "I bet it's that bloody compost." That triggered a nasty thought. "Oh, God... Is everyone's plot like this?" Curiosity led him to the end of his plot. On tiptoes, he peered over the fence. "Oh, good God... It looks like a bloody Hammer Horror film."

Thick mist drifted low over the rows of cabbages and turnips, and patches of the strange light lit up the ground. Jim half expected Boris Karloff to come stomping out of the petunias.

Over the operatic bombast of Wagner coming from his radio, Jim could hear what sounded like movement, a glutinous slurp like something crawling through mud. Taking his half-moon spectacles from his pocket and placing them on his nose, he squinted over towards Mr Wingate's cabbages. It looked as though the cabbages were moving. Jim shook his head and rubbed his weary eyes, certain that it must have been some kind of illusion caused by the mist.

"James Robert Matthews! Get your body down here this instant!"

Jim's already fraught nerves were irreparably shredded by the sudden shrill shriek. "Oh, hell, it's the wife!"

He didn't need to see the look on her face to know he was in trouble. Nobody ever uses your full name unless you're in some really deep manure. He cursed as he glanced at his wristwatch. He was two hours late for dinner. In all the excitement, he'd completely lost track of time and his wife had been having kittens. She'd been convinced, as many women with retired husbands often were, that he'd gone to the shed and shuffled off his mortal coil.

Jim took one last look at the strange scene before locking up the shed and heading down the hill towards what would prove to be a world-class guilt trip. Marjorie was a master at the ancient art of dishing out a good rollicking. She would have made a superb Sunday school teacher.

Jim bit the bullet and apologised profusely. His survival instincts had kicked in, and he decided that a heartfelt mea culpa was the way to go. And it worked. After eating dinner in silence, Marjorie went off the boil and retired to the front room to curl up in front of the TV.

While his wife watched a reality show that made him want to claw his own eyes out, Jim sat and ruminated on the strange events of the evening. Staring at the sad-looking cactus on the windowsill, he decided to mount a full investigation into the horticultural mystery by the warm light of day. He briefly contemplated telling his wife about what he'd seen but swiftly thought better of it. The mood she was in, she would probably have frog-marched him down to the nearest mental health facility.

No, if he was going to get to the bottom of this mystery, he would need some specialist help. And he knew just the woman for the job.

🍅

Dr Ruth Jenkins had one eye pressed to a microscope when the door to the scientific research centre just outside Betyls Cove received a vigorous knocking.

"Oh, sodding hell… What now?"

She sighed. Ruth hated flower show season with a passion. It was a non-stop nightmare of interruptions. Not only was she a biologist of high esteem with a focus on unusual flora, but she was also a member of the royal horticultural society, *and* one of the judges.

She cursed softly under her breath and considered pretending she wasn't in.

"If that's another old dear with a pot of drooping tulips, or an old boy with a rudely-shaped carrot, I'm going to scream."

Begrudgingly removing the fascinating kelp sample from the scope, she switched on the lights. Running a hand through her glossy black hair, Ruth exhaled and awaited the oncoming storm.

The face at the grilled window of the mobile office was *not* one she would have ever expected.

"Hello, Jim. You're the last person I expected to see."

In the twenty-plus years she'd lived in the area, not once had Jim bothered her with carrot trouble.

"Well," Jim began hesitantly. "Normally, I wouldn't bother you. I know you must be busy and all. But something weird is happening over at the allotments."

"Weird?" Ruth cocked an eyebrow. "How weird are we talking?"

"Really bloody weird, and I figured you'd be the only person who might be able to make head or tail of it." Jim paused to compose himself. "You see, I was up there last night, and the ground was...glowing."

Ruth gave him a puzzled look. "Glowing?"

"Aye. Look, I know it sounds daft, but the flowerbeds

were lit up like bloody Christmas trees. There was this mist too. Stunk something awful, it did. Like the bins 'round the back of the abattoir."

"Bloody hell," Ruth gasped. "That doesn't sound good."

"Yeah, it didn't seem natural. I think it has something to do with Mick Bradshaw's compost."

"Oh, for fuck's sake!" Ruth snapped, before realising Jim's surprise. "Oh, sorry, Jim! It's just, that man is a royal pain in the backside. What's he been peddling now?"

"It's a new type of compost that makes things grow really quickly. I put some on my marrows, and they tripled in size within a couple of weeks."

Ruth looked pensive. "Well, that isn't natural... I'll have to take a look at these marrows of yours."

"I thought you might want a sample, so I've got one out in the car."

"Jim, you're a bloody marvel. I don't suppose you brought any of the compost, did you?"

"I have," Jim beamed. Ever a practical man, and remembering the Boy Scout motto, Jim had dug up a marrow and put some of the surrounding soil in an old gravy granules pot before driving over. "I'll go and fetch them."

He pootled outside and returned in under a minute, lugging the now-massive marrow. Finding space on the bench, he placed it down and let Ruth take a look.

"Blimey, that is a corker. You're telling me that this has tripled in size in just a couple of weeks?"

"Yeah, I have the measurements right here," Jim said, producing a battered old notebook and a pencil stub from the pocket of his body warmer. "If you look here..." and he pointed to a distinct line of colour separation on the vegetable, "...you can see where the new growth meets the old."

Ruth gazed at the strangely bloated marrow with a puzzled look on her face. "This is unbelievable..." she breathed. "Nothing should cause this kind of growth in such a short space of time. Unless... Oh, crap."

Her green eyes widened in alarm, and she hurried over to the equipment store.

"Unless what?" Jim asked, a hint of panic in his voice.

Momentarily, Ruth returned with a box that gave out a steady click.

"Crikey... Is that a Geiger counter?"

As Ruth passed the needle over the swollen marrow, she let out a sigh of relief. "Sorry to alarm you, Jim. I just had a horrible thought. But it's clean. Nothing to worry about."

"Thank the Lord for that." Jim sighed, steadying himself on the worktop. "If it isn't radioactive, then..."

"Then I have no idea." She removed her glasses and buffed them with a microfibre cloth from her pocket. "I don't like having no idea. Pass me the compost sample."

Jim produced the repurposed pot and handed it to her.

"Ta. Could you do me a favour?"

"Yeah, sure. Anything.

Ruth sighed. "I could murder a cuppa. Any chance you could make me one. There's a kettle and tea bags in the kitchen out the back."

"With pleasure," Jim smiled. "I'm a little bit parched myself."

Jim was a firm believer that any problem, no matter how dire, could be overcome with a good cup of tea, so he set about his task with gusto.

Ruth gazed into her microscope for what could have been hours while Jim busied himself brewing tea and washing slides. Never once had he ever thought he'd become a lab assistant at his ripe old age. The thought made him smile. It looked like you could teach an old dog new tricks after all.

With every passing minute, Ruth's expression darkened. She tutted and bit her lip, before whipping her head around and glaring at Jim with horror in her eyes. "How much of this stuff is out there?"

"I dunno. A lot, I think. Why? What's wrong?"

"This isn't just compost. There's something else in the sample, some kind of living organism. Did Mick say where he got it from?"

Jim's brow knitted in concentration as he desperately tried to recall their conversation. "He did. Hold on; it'll come to me."

Ruth continued while his gears turned. "You see, until now, I've only ever seen this kind of growth in the so-called Pluto Cap. It's a mushroom that grows in the sea cave under the Crag. This compost has the same kind of strange cell structure as those mushrooms."

Jim snapped his fingers in triumph. "That's it. Mick said this stuff came from the cave."

"Crap," Ruth said flatly. "Then whatever has been causing the strange properties in those mushrooms has now spread to other flora."

"Is that a bad thing?" Jim asked. "I mean, if it doesn't harm anyone, couldn't it combat world hunger?"

Ruth shook her head. "I'm not sure it *is* harmless. I mean, the Pluto cap is a mutated strain of the liberty cap mushroom—Psilocybe Semilanceata—and it already possesses the poisonous qualities inherent in the genus, so it's hard to say for sure. The Pluto Cap is *wildly* dangerous. I'll have to run some tests on that marrow of yours."

"Go for it," Jim said. "This is the runt of the litter anyhow. The others are *much* bigger."

"You're kidding? Bigger than *this*?"

"Oh, yeah," Jim said, with a mixture of pride and concern. "Some of them are ruddy huge."

Ruth shook her head again and reached for a long, serrated knife. "Hold it steady, would you?"

"Sure."

Jim firmly grasped his marrow with both hands as she got to work. A rancid odour belched forth from the gigantic cucurbit. Ruth gagged and Jim retched as the marrow split open. What poured forth from the centre of the marrow was straight from a charnel house nightmare, a foetid collection of part-digested flesh and small animal bones.

Ruth stepped back from the bench and grimaced. "Well, I think it's safe to say that nobody will be eating that."

CHAPTER 4

"But...how the hell did the animals get in there?" Jim asked, as he drove back to town with Ruth in the passenger seat. "It's not like a marrow has a mouth."

"I have no idea," Ruth admitted, "but they were definitely the bones of small rodents. Mice, rats, maybe even rabbits, and they were *definitely* inside your marrow, so... We have to assume they were consumed somehow."

After they'd recovered from the initial shock of the disgusting sludge pouring onto Ruth's bench, the duo had decided that all the soil and flora tainted by the compost had to be collected up and destroyed. They had no idea how far the taint had spread, nor how many gardeners were using the contaminated compost, but they knew a man who did.

Mick Bradshaw lived on the outskirts of town in a dilapidated farmhouse with his wife, Jane, and her ever-growing clowder of cats. Their only son had flown the nest many years before, and Mrs Bradshaw had filled the void with felines. Around town, Mick was known as something of a rogue, and his wife as the crazy cat lady of Betyls Cove. Together they made quite the pair.

"Right, here we are."

Jim edged the car carefully up the muddy driveway and came to a stop next to a rusty, old tractor. A light burned in one of the upstairs windows. Other than that, there was no sign of life. He felt a creeping sense of disquiet upon noticing that there was no sign of Mick's chickens, his faithful dog, Rex, or a single moggy.

Ruth stepped from the passenger seat and squelched into the mud. Looking around, she also felt uneasy. It was far too quiet for a farm, even one as half-arsed as Mick Bradshaw's.

"Let's try the house first," she said, motioning to the stout front door, hanging ajar and swinging gently in the breeze.

"Good plan," Jim agreed, as they walked up the path to the door. "Hello? Mick, Jane, you in there?"

"Maybe they're round the back?" Ruth whispered. "I'll take a look."

Jim nodded and banged on the door. "Hello?"

His voice echoed around the high-ceilinged interior as he called through the crack. Upon receiving no answer, he pushed the door open. The weather bleached wood creaked on rusty hinges as it swung inward. Upon hearing no sounds from within, he called out one last time before stepping inside.

The air was heavy and stale like nothing had moved inside for days. A rank odour drifted from the rear of the building, tickling Jim's nasal hairs. Walking through the front room, Jim headed out into the kitchen. Instantly, he located the source of the powerful aroma. A cloud of black flies buzzed around a large stew pot. Its contents had been left to spoil in the warm summer weather and had quickly rotted. Maggots writhed and squirmed over the disgusting contents. In the dim light, Jim could make out a faint glow radiating from the pot.

"Shit…" he whispered.

It looked as though the Bradshaws had been eating the tainted vegetables. As Jim turned, a clattering noise from the back of the room gave him a start.

"Sorry," came a voice. "I knocked an old watering can over."

It was Ruth. She had made her way around and entered the back door.

"Found anyone yet?"

"No, but it looks like they've been eating the produce. Mick was bragging about his wife's tomatoes…"

"Oh god," Ruth whispered. "We need to find them quickly… You check upstairs. I'll check the outbuildings."

"Righto."

Jim turned and took the door to the staircase.

Ruth walked back out of the kitchen door…

The setting sun, hanging low over the craggy hills, dazzled Ruth as she left through the back door. The yard at the rear was a mess of clutter. Rusting farm machinery and car parts sat entangled in a formidable jungle of weeds that had lain untended for years, maybe even decades. Avoiding the debris, she trudged through the mire of mud and pig muck towards the barn.

Mick had very little livestock these days, and the three pigs he owned had lived in a converted end of the barn since their sty had been flattened by the gales coming off Bodmin Moor. The first thing that struck her was the smell. Not just the usual fruity aroma that pigs created, but something much more terrible. Her scalp prickled with unease. Her hand shook as she reached out and pushed one of the large doors aside. The smell was even worse now, and instantly recognisable. The cloying stench of death.

Steeling herself, Ruth continued to push the doors open until the gap was wide enough to enter. It took her eyes a second or two to adjust to the change in light. Motes of dust twisted in the narrow shafts of sunlight sneaking through the cracks in the barn wall. Once she could see, Ruth looked around the cluttered interior. One side of the barn was filled with stacks of hay bales and piles of junk, the other...

"Oh, God..." Ruth gasped, as she located the source of the smell. "Poor things."

The pigs were dead. Hesitantly, she moved in for a closer look. The same mist that Jim had described hung low over the pen, and all the vegetable stalks, off-cuts and peelings that made up a pig's diet bloomed with the preternatural glow. Ruth's analytical mind quickly deduced that the pigs had died from ingesting the tainted vegetables.

"What the hell?"

Ruth swatted at the bloated, black flies circling the three carcasses as she peered over the side of the makeshift sty. At first, she thought it was a trick of the light, but soon realised that the dead pigs were giving off the same indescribable radiance as the vegetation. Ruth had to fight against a rising tide of bile upon spotting grotesquely bloated, glowing maggots wriggling in the eye sockets. When a particularly bulbous specimen fell out of the pig's snout, she had to look away. It was too much.

"Jesus, Mick, what have you done?"

Clamping her hand firmly over her mouth Ruth started to turn away when a strange movement caught her eye. The bellies of the deceased porkers were moving ever so slightly.

"What the...?"

As she tried to deduce the source of the movement, it came again, stronger this time.

"That's no maggot."

Ruth bit her lip. Her palms were clammy, her throat tight. It was as though a snake or gigantic worm was straining its head against the thick skin in an attempt to break free. Ruth was transfixed by the unnatural movement. It reminded her of someone poking their finger through a rubber glove. The skin strained and grew taut.

Splat!

Ruth let out a yelp of shock and revulsion as the belly of the swine ripped asunder. Putrid ichor showered her lab coat, turning the white fabric a disgusting brownish-red. A strange tendril flicked from the gaping wound and swung in the air. Ruth recoiled as it lashed towards her, slapping the side of the pigpen. She screamed as several more of the writhing appendages burst from the three dead little pigs.

Backing away, Ruth's foot caught on an old spade handle that had been hidden under a pile of straw. She tumbled, losing her balance and landing flat on her backside. The largest of the tendrils rose above the pen and loomed over her. Its end was needle-sharp and poised to puncture her abdomen.

At the last second, she managed to scramble out of its trajectory. It cracked like a whip and slammed into the floor. Ruth got to her feet and backed towards the door, never taking her eyes off her attacker. The tendril burrowed deep into the earthen floor of the barn. Turning at the last moment, she slipped through the door and slammed it shut.

Ruth looked towards the house with panic rising in her chest. "Roots... That's what they were, fucking roots!"

🎃🎃🎃

Every step Jim took on the old staircase croaked like a disgruntled toad. He mused that Jane Bradshaw hadn't been much of a housekeeper as his shoulder brushed against a row of grime-crusted picture frames. A dusty cobweb hung from the light-fitting, peppered with dead flies and moulted spider exoskeletons. The air was even thicker up here. He could almost chew it.

Upon reaching the landing, he stepped into the master bedroom. The curtains were drawn, and the light was switched off, but still, there was a glow. *That* glow.

Mist rolled off the bed and across the floor. Jim's mouth fell open in shock as he saw what was growing out of the bed. A mass of vegetation spread out over the double mattress, and from it grew a grotesquely twisted tree. The leaves were large, flat, white, and waxy. They oozed a foul liquid, as though they were sweating.

At the base of the tree, were two lumps of torn and twisted meat wrapped in a bed-sheet. Human cadavers. Roots had punctured the bodies, coiling around the bones, mangling the muscles and rendering them unrecognisable. Only a large tuft of ginger beard poking out from under the rancid sheet identified them.

"Mick, no!"

Jim shook his head and caught a sob in the back of his throat. He took in the full horror of the botanic monstrosity. Its bone-like branches twisted upwards, reaching towards the window like a skeletal claw. It was desperate to grow, to consume everything in its path.

The tree throbbed and pulsed, bathing the room in its unearthly illumination. Jim's mind reeled. He couldn't believe that what he was looking at was the Bradshaws. It was too horrific to be true.

The mist drifted up to Jim's throat, stinking like a cesspit, hammering his gag reflex. He choked. Alerted by the noise, the tree burst into life, branches twisting around its trunk, making a grab for Jim's head.

"Bloody Hell!"

He flailed backwards, shoulder clipping the door frame, and landed hard on his back, driving the air from his lungs.

As he wheezed and gagged, there was a piercing hiss from the bedroom. A tendril shot from the body of the growth and coiled itself around his wellington boot. His fingers raked the flock wallpaper as he struggled to pull himself clear. His free foot banged against the thin dividing wall, causing one of the pictures to fall. It bounced off the bannister, shattering and showering him in filthy shards of glass.

Jim struggled to keep the tree from reeling him in like a gigantic, geriatric salmon. His hand fell onto a jagged sliver of glass. Displaying bendiness not usual in one of his advanced years, he twisted his torso and lashed out at the vicious vine. As the glass cut into the thrashing root, the tree hissed and growled. He hacked at it with every ounce of strength in his body. Eventually, a mighty crack announced that Jim was finally free. The severed tendril whipped around in pain, spraying Jim with a black substance that smelled like it had come directly from Satan's toilet.

Getting to his feet, Jim half-slid, half-ran down the stairs. At the bottom, he slammed into a small table, sending an overgrown aspidistra crashing to the floor, vase shattered. Jim's breath came in ragged heaves, heart hammering like crazy as he fought the urge to collapse. Through force of will alone, he managed to control his jelly legs. Using the wall for support, he wobbled out into the corridor.

Jim was starting to compose himself when a catastrophic crash jolted his attention violently towards the living room. A wide crack spread across the ceiling, the plaster sagged, and the old wooden beams buckled. Another impact sent a plume of dust and plaster raining down over the floral-patterned sofa. One, final crash sent the three flying ducks on the wall spinning to the ground as a massive rent appeared in the ceiling above. Jim cried out as a mass of roots thrust through the gap, spilling into the room like snakes.

"Holy shit!" Jim bellowed, gathering whatever strength he had remaining in his tired body and making a mad dash for the back door.

As the fading sunlight blinded him once again, he screamed in panic as he collided with something on the threshold. The object he crashed into screamed back. It was the terror-stricken body of Ruth Jenkins.

"P-plant monsters!" Jim stammered, struggling to force the words from his lips.

Ruth nodded. "I know. It's the same in the barn. Any sign of Mick?"

Jim nodded sadly and gestured towards the thing in the living room.

"Fuck. Right, I'm calling the rozzers. We're going to need all the help we can get."

CHAPTER 5

"*H*a ha, that's a good one, Doc. Plant monsters!*" The voice on the other end of the phone burst into a fit of hysterical laughter. *"You been experimenting with the Pluto Cap again?"*

"I'm not joking! The Brads—" Ruth abruptly stopped talking and turned to Jim with a look of disbelief on her face. "The pig-headed idiot hung up on me!"

She huffed and slammed her phone on the dashboard of Jim's car.

"It looks like we'll have to deal with this ourselves," Jim said wearily.

Ruth had bandaged his hand and cleaned up his scuffs and scrapes using the first aid kit he kept under his passenger seat. He was currently enjoying a medicinal brandy from his hip flask.

"Yeah," Ruth sighed, "We need to destroy the specimens. We can't let this thing spread. If this gets loose... Well, let's just say that it wouldn't be good."

They had filled each other in on their respective horrors, then regrouped at the car. They had seen no further movement from either the barn or the house. Still, they looked around themselves jumpily, like a pair of paranoid meerkats.

"I reckon fire is the way to go." Ruth nodded to herself. "Did you spot anything flammable in the house?"

"I saw a bottle of whiskey in the kitchen. I wasn't really looking."

"It's a start..." Ruth paused as a light bulb went off over her head. "There were a couple of jerry cans over by the barn. We could siphon the tractor and these old cars. We'd have enough fuel to burn Rome, never mind a small farm."

Jim nodded and hauled himself out of the car. Pain shot down his spine as he straightened. With a cocked eyebrow, he gazed at the glorious sunset, noting the irony. The old country saying, 'Red sky at night, shepherd's delight', was often twisted by townies into, 'Red sky at night, barn on fire'.

Once the brandy had worked its magic and both of them had caught their breath, they left the safety of the vehicle and commenced searching for flammable liquids. The two jerry cans were full of petrol, and Jim found several bottles of paraffin in a storage shed used for lighting bonfires and barbecues. It seemed that Mick had been, fortunately, something of a pyromaniac.

Suitably armed, they decided to tackle the barn first.

Jim loaded one of the cans onto a wheelbarrow and trundled it inside the foetid barn while Ruth stood guard with a pitchfork and badging hook, in case the roots got frisky again. For now, they were still. Odd-looking shoots had started to reach up from the rotting swine, entwining and growing at an alarming rate. Soon, there would be three more tree-creatures to deal with.

The barn floor was covered in straw, hay and wood-shavings, and it would go up in seconds once lit, so they need-ed to reach a safe distance before ignition. Getting close enough to the growth was the biggest problem. Every time they neared the foul mass, the thing would start to shake, and its tendrils would tense, preparing to lash out.

After a few minutes of fruitless advance, Jim had an idea. "Ruth," he hissed, not wanting to excite the growth. "I spotted some guttering propped up against the outside loo. Could you go and grab it for me?"

"Yeah, no problem," Ruth replied. "Are you sure you'll be okay in here alone?"

"I think so, as long as I keep my distance." Jim indicated a corner of the barn piled with junk. "I'm going to make a torch with that old broom handle and those old rags over there so we can light it."

"Right, I won't be a minute."

Ruth turned and hurried from the barn, grateful for the burst of fresh, clean country air. She crossed the yard, dodging old tyres and off-cuts of barbed wire, then sprinted in the direction of the tumble-down outside toilet.

Leaning against the crumbling convenience, amongst a pile of split, corrugated UPVC sheets and mangled chicken wire, was the guttering Jim had spotted. The cluster of dis-carded items was overgrown with nettles and infested with garden spiders. Ruth didn't have time to worry about the odd cobweb or sting, however, and bravely reached inside to grab the guttering.

Brushing a mass of cobwebs and dead insects off her filthy lab coat, she turned to head back towards the barn.

Something strange in the corner of her eye caught her attention.

"What the living fuck?"

Inside the greenhouse was a nightmare, but...

"First things first, Ruth." Jim needed her, so she didn't have time to worry about it right then. "We'll deal with that later."

🍊🎃🍊

After Ruth left the barn, Jim cautiously crossed to the corner and selected a broom handle. He was in the process of gathering up some rags and hairy, orange bailing twine when he nearly jumped through the roof. The buzzing of the flies, and the general horror of the situation, had already got his nerves jangling like a Morris dancer's bells. So, when a brute of a brown rat emerged, screeching in anger, from its hiding place amongst the junk, he nearly had a coronary.

"Go on, bugger off!" Jim snarled, swiping at the furry brute with the broom handle.

It scurried away, but he was far too old to be sparring with unruly rodents and had to take a minute to get his breathing under control. Once his hands had stopped shaking, Jim began wrapping rags around the end of the broom and binding it with the twine.

As he focused on the task at hand, he was blissfully unaware of the encroaching peril.

The commotion both he and the rat had made during their brief scuffle seemed to have awoken the evil plant. As Jim fussed with a rag, a root pushed itself up from the barn floor and started to slither towards him. Its pointy tip tasted the air, worm-like in its movements as it threaded silently through the debris and dirt.

"Bugger," Jim cursed, as a splinter punctured his index finger.

As his hand shot back, he fumbled the broom handle and it clattered to the floor. The root paused as Jim bent to pick it up. Coiling itself on the spot like a cobra, it gave itself enough length to strike. Straightening back up, Jim commenced tightly knotting the twine. The root tensed, ready.

"Jim, look out!" Ruth yelled, giving him yet another start. How many more his ticker could withstand was anybody's guess.

Ruth dropped the guttering and pounced across the barn in a stunning display of feline dexterity. With a roar, she brought the sickle down on the deadly root, slicing it cleanly in two before it could pierce Jim's calf.

He stumbled out of the way as a jet of filth spewed from the severed root. Ruth jumped back to her feet. Clamping her hand on Jim's shoulder, she guided him out of harm's way and back towards the wheelbarrow.

"I think it's best if you let me pour the petrol, don't you?" She smiled on noting the tremulousness of Jim's hands. "Turn the barrow around and hold the guttering steady."

"Okay. Good call."

Jim turned and positioned the barrow as close to the growth as he dared, then held the guttering tight against the highest point of the barrow. He angled the half-pipe towards the pigsty. As Ruth poured the flammable liquid, it flowed directly towards it. Fuel splashed the wooden pen and pooled around it, seeping under and through towards the pigs. The plant puffed out more of its noxious mist.

It knew what they were doing. It was aware. It whipped its roots violently in their direction in an attempt to stop them.

Once enough petrol had doused the plant, they removed the wheelbarrow and laid a trail of fuel away from the pen to within chucking distance. Finally, Ruth kicked the can over, allowing the remainder of the liquid to flow freely, and ran out of the barn. Jim doused the makeshift torch in the lighter fluid, then joined her outside the door.

Jim patted each pocket of his body-warmer in turn and finally located his lighter. He had quit smoking years ago, but had never gotten out of the habit of carrying a lighter. The first two flicks of the flint did nothing but dislodge the pocket fluff clogging the guard. Jim swore under his breath. The third flick produced ignition. The torch exploded into life and nearly singed the peak of his flat cap.

"Stand back," Ruth said. "This is going to be fierce."

She took the torch and sent it in a graceful arc towards the pooling petrol with an underarm throw. With a roar, the petrol fumes exploded into life. The force of the blast ruptured the pig carcasses, splattering the barn wall with gore. Flames engulfed the rear portion of the barn, and the plant emitted a high-pitched wail that had no effect on Jim but caused Ruth to blanch in pain as they ran across the yard in the direction of Jim's vehicle.

After reaching a safe distance from the inferno, Jim

exhaled deeply. "Well, that wasn't so hard," he said, with a sarcastic wink. "One down, one more to go."

As Jim gripped the wheelbarrow and turned towards the house, Ruth stopped him with a hand on his bony shoulder.

"Hold that thought, Jim," she said, voice exuding dread. "I think you should see the greenhouse…"

ᗆ🎃ᗇ

The windows of the old greenhouse were thick with condensation, mud and bird droppings, lending a touch of the psychedelic to the strange, pulsating light from within. Jim and Ruth approached warily and pushed the door aside with the fork-handle.

"Christ, what a stink!" Jim choked, as a wall of mist greeted them at the door.

Ruth retched and pulled the stained collar of her lab coat over her mouth and nose. "Get back. Don't breathe it in."

The mist rolled out of the door and over the raised beds, pushing them back from the weathered structure. Jim and Ruth retreated to the car and waited for the strong Cornish winds to clear the air.

Once the mist had dissipated somewhat, Ruth peered inside.

"Bloody hell… I used to watch *Attack of the Killer Tomatoes* when I was at Uni, but this is taking the piss!"

Jim's mouth worked, but no sound came out. Before them lay several horrific parodies of tomato plants. Their leaves were slimy and leprous, covered with thick, bristly hairs. The stems were twisted beyond all recognition, and more closely resembled a diseased strain of coral or cave plant than something that bore fruit.

"Well, he wasn't kidding about the size of his wife's tomatoes," Jim said wryly.

The fruits were disgustingly bloated and had swollen to the size of large pumpkins. The strange glow radiated from them as they pulsed like evil tumours.

"Pass me the pitchfork," Ruth said.

Jim complied and handed her the tool. She reached towards one of the larger fruits and gently poked it with one of the sharp prongs. The skin burst, releasing more of the mist. Jim and Ruth gagged in horror as a collection of bones, half-digested meat, feathers, and matted tufts of fur tumbled from it like a charnel waterfall.

"Well," Ruth said, between gasps, "I think we know what happened to the cats and chickens."

Jim bolted from the greenhouse, forcibly blowing the foul stench from his nose. He hastened across the raised beds, trampling beetroot and carrots. The sun was nearly down by now, and traversing the chaotic vegetable garden was tricky in the fading light. Reaching the wheelbarrow, he gathered up as many bottles of lighter fluid as he could carry and a bundle of rags.

Since the popping of the fruit, the plant had become agitated, furious. Ruth had backed away from the door and was in the process of fending off an attacking vine with her sickle. She yelped and cursed as she flailed at the attacking plant. Jim couldn't believe his eyes when he returned. It looked like she was fencing with a bush.

He uncapped the bottles and stuffed them with rags. "Quick, over here!"

Ruth backed away from her sap-filled sparring partner and joined Jim on the flowerbed.

"Here... I'll light 'em, you chuck 'em."

Jim passed the first bottle to Ruth and touched the flame of his lighter to the paraffin-soaked rag.

Ruth sent the makeshift firebomb spinning towards its target. It connected with the base of one of the stems and burst, showering the terrible tomato plant with flames. As she threw the second bottle, the plants emitted a high-pitched, almost ultra-sonic wail. The greenhouse shattered, and as the third flaming bottle found its target, burst outwards, blowing jagged shards in Jim and Ruth's direction.

"Down!" Ruth yelled, and threw Jim facedown into the mud.

She covered her head just in time, as the bulbous tomatoes ruptured and exploded. The mist caught the flames, and the greenhouse was annihilated.

The plant burned, withered and drooped as Jim attempted to get to his feet. Ruth noticed the man's struggle and gently assisted him.

"Are you okay, Jim?" she asked. "Sorry about that... I didn't really want you being roasted alive."

"Don't worry about me," Jim coughed, as he dusted himself down. "I owe you my life...and the life of my flat cap."

He smiled, shaking dirt and glass fragments from his treasured hat. Jim straightened up and winced as a twinge of sciatica shot down his leg.

"Anyway, my doctor has been saying that I don't get enough exercise."

Ruth laughed and brushed the muck from her hair. "I take it that the gas or whatever these things produce is combustible then. Methane, most likely." She took a pair of tweezers from her coat pocket and got to work on a nasty glass splinter that had become embedded in her thumb. "Just the house to go then..."

"Yep," Jim replied wearily. "The house was full of that mist, so it'll go up like a rocket when we light it. I still have a bottle of firelighter left. I think we should pour the petrol in from the back of the house like we did in the barn, then lob a Molotov through the front window."

Ruth exhaled in relief as she pulled the splinter from her hand. "Sounds like a wise plan."

🍅🎃🍅

As luck would have it, both of the front windows were open. Jim carefully poured petrol from the kitchen, down the guttering, into the front room. The root system had been growing at a tremendous rate and, by now, had almost swallowed the room. The mist hung low, shrouding the floor.

Ruth had Jim retreat to a safe distance before carefully lighting the bottle of paraffin. Skilfully, she tossed the bottle, and its volatile contents, through the open window. Ruth didn't look back. She simply covered her head with her hands and raced into the garage by the gate where Jim waited.

The farmhouse did indeed go up like a rocket. Rubble, slate, and glass were scattered into the night sky. Several smaller explosions rocked the residence, reducing it to a smouldering pile of wreckage in a matter of minutes. The horrific growth had been exterminated.

Jim and Ruth ducked under the hanging garage door into a night lit by three separate pyres. Slowly, they turned and walked back to Jim's vehicle. Just as they were about to get in the car and drive away, a police car screeched to a halt across their path, blocking their escape.

"Great," Ruth muttered. "*Now* the police arrive."

"Yeah, just as we've committed three counts of arson." Jim shook his head. "I'm far too old for an ASBO."

The car's engine switched off, the exhaust ticking as the cool air hit it. The passenger door opened, and instead of the expected uniformed constable, a little old lady in a tweed overcoat and a crochet bobble-hat stepped out. Jim and Ruth looked at each other in acute befuddlement.

The driver's door burst open with so much force that it nearly flew off its hinges as Detective Sergeant Finch struggled to extract himself from the car. The man-mountain was jammed in like a cork. Once free, he smoothed out his rumpled suit, then stroked his thick walrus moustache.

"In danger of being a bloody cliché: 'Ello, 'ello, 'ello. What's goin' on 'ere then?" he boomed, doing his best *Dixon of Dock Green* impersonation.

Jim stammered. "Well, erm, you see... It's like this..."

Ruth chimed in, trying to help her accomplice. "You're probably not going to believe this…"

"I don't know," Finch cut in. "After what I've seen today, I'm ready to believe just about anything." He turned to the elderly woman standing beside his car. "Ain't that right, Mum?"

CHAPTER 6

Ivy Finch, chairwoman of the Betyls Cove Women's Institute and green-fingered guru, opened up the garden centre at the crack of dawn as usual. The septuagenarian was a force to be reckoned with and had point-blank refused to retire. The way she saw it, she would still be gardening at home, so she may as well be getting paid for it.

The day had started quite typically, with a few cups of tea and a good natter with Edith in the canteen. She had followed this by laying out some bedding plants in the greenhouse. All was right with the world until just after lunchtime, when everything took a distinctly bizarre turn.

After polishing off a cheese scone and a cream tea, Ivy sat down for fifteen minutes with the Guardian crossword. The calm was dispelled by Jean Young—one of her WI cohorts—hurrying, ashen-faced, into the canteen. "Oh, Ivy!" she crooned. "Have you heard the awful news?"

"No, what news?" Ivy asked, brushing Rich Tea crumbs off her chin. "Whatever is the matter, dear?"

"It's terrible," Jean gabbled. "Absolutely terrible. Poor Mrs Wilson has just dropped dead in her conservatory. I found the body!"

She wailed, pulling at the corners of a tear-sodden

handkerchief. Ivy put a tender, liver-spotted hand on her shoulder and coaxed her to sit down.

"Try to calm down, dear," she said soothingly. "I'll get Edith to make you a cup of hot, sweet tea."

Ivy waved a well-practised hand signal at Edith, who quickly started brewing up. Ivy was something of an agony aunt for the town, the garden centre canteen her consultation room, and Edith her anaesthetist.

"Drink that, dear. It'll do you a world of good." Edith purred as she placed the china cup and saucer down in front of Jean. "Biscuit?"

She offered a packet of Rich Tea. Jean shook her head and took a slurp of the milky beverage.

Ivy smiled benignly, showing off her gleaming dentures. "Now, what's all this about Patty then, love?"

Behind the wire-rimmed spectacles perched on her aquiline nose, tears were welling up in Jean's pale, blue eyes. "Well," she began. "I popped over to her house on my way to the church. I wanted to see how she was getting on with the bake for the summer fete. I knocked on the door but got no answer. I figured she must have been out in the garden or pottering around in her conservatory. But when I got there and looked through the window, there she was, on her back in the middle of the floor, face blue as a baboon's rump."

"Oh, no..." Ivy gasped. "Poor Patty. Whatever did you do?"

"I was shaken, as you would imagine, but I tried the door. It was open, so I went inside and checked for a pulse. She was cold as a polar bear's toes." Edith paused to wet her lips with a sip of tea. "Anyway, that was when I called the ambulance."

"What did they say happened?" Edith, who'd been hovering around the table, asked.

"Well, that's the odd thing..." Jean paused for dramatic effect. "They say that she asphyxiated. That she suffered a fatal asthma attack, but... Patty didn't have asthma."

Ivy arched a wispy grey eyebrow quizzically. "What the Dickens was it then?"

Jean leaned forward, whispering so the two men on the adjacent table couldn't hear. "She had pollen around her nose. Thick pollen."

"Pollen?" Ivy and Edith asked, in unison.

"From the flowers she was arranging for the fete," Jean continued. "The paramedic said it looked like she died of hay fever!"

"Poppycock!" Ivy spat. "Killer hayfever? That's utterly ridiculous, Some of these nurses, pah! I don't know. Their medical license isn't worth the paper it's printed on. Back in my day—"

"It could have been an extreme allergic reaction," Edith cut in. "You know, anaphylaxis or something."

"Hmm..." Ivy mused. "Okay, that's possible, thank you. That makes more sense. What was she arranging, Jean dear?"

"I'm not quite sure. I didn't recognise them. They looked a bit like dahlias, but bigger. Fatter." Jean took another slurp of tea. "Strange-looking."

Edith peered at Jean like a member of the Spanish Inquisition. "Define 'strange-looking.'"

"Hold on." Ivy flapped her hand in Edith's direction. "Did you say dahlias?" Not waiting for Jean to respond, Ivy continued with a tinge of hysteria in her voice. "Patty gave us some exotic dahlias a few days ago to put in the greenhouse. The manager wanted to take some cuttings!"

Suddenly, as if on cue, a piercing cry came from the direction of the plant nursery at the rear of the building. Jean yelped and dropped her tea in shock, shattering the china cup.

Ivy leapt to her feet. "What in several types of fertilizer is going on?"

As the trio watched, open-mouthed, a wave of people came rushing from the greenhouse area. They were all coughing, spluttering and choking.

"Ruddy hell!" Edith rounded on the two young girls at the cash register. "Don't just stand there gawping. Call a sodding ambulance!"

Ivy and Edith rushed towards the nursery with Jean trailing along behind, puffing and panting. Her ample frame wasn't built for sprinting. As they neared the nursery greenhouse, they saw a dense miasma of glowing pollen swirling above the carefully laid out displays. Ivy paused and held out her arms to halt her friends.

"Wait! You heard what Jean said. This stuff is deadly." Her roving green eyes landed on a display next to one of the help desks. "Over here. Grab one of these."

She scuttled over and wrestled an industrial grade dust mask from its polythene wrapper. Stretching the elastic straps over her ears, she turned and nodded as the others followed suit. Once suitably protected, they entered the greenhouse.

The heat inside the cavernous nursery was stifling. Sunlight streamed through the glass, catching dancing motes of thick, yellow pollen in its rays. Cautiously, the three ladies made their way down through the rows of seedlings in grow bags towards Patty's mutant dahlias.

"Crikey," Janice said. "Look at the size of the blasted things. The heads are like bin lids!"

The three women stared in a mixture of wonder and horror at the sight of the gigantic plants, their stems as thick as a man's leg. Each flower shuddered almost imperceptibly, vibrating faster than the human eye could keep up with. Petals danced with colours of an unnatural hue. The effect was hypnotic. Jean stepped towards the nearest flower, entranced by the mysterious bloom.

"For God's sake, Jean!" Ivy hollered. "Keep back, you daft bugger!"

The flower drew its petals inwards as though taking a deep breath, then puffed a stream of viscid pollen in Jean's face. The startled woman staggered, clawing at her face mask in a desperate attempt to clear a breathing hole. The rancid substance quickly congealed, creating an impenetrable barrier.

"Edith!" Ivy commanded, tearing the mask off her friend's ears. "Get her out of here! Now!"

Edith manhandled Jean by her flabby shoulders, steering her out of the greenhouse.

While Ivy was distracted, one of the daemonic dahlias

moved into a firing position. She noticed it from the corner of her eye and spun around to face her attacker. Darting left and right, Ivy tried to keep out of range. Her every movement was matched by the killer flower.

Taking cover behind a display, Ivy grabbed a bottle of max-strength weedkiller off a nearby shelf, twisted the nozzle to stream and opened fire. A jet of liquid struck the monstrous bloom in the centre of its bloated body. It writhed in pain, steaming and giving off a foul odour. It was like some kind of weird chemistry experiment gone awry. In seconds the stem had withered, drooped, then fallen to the linoleum floor, defeated.

The other dahlias started to jet out streams of pollen in Ivy's direction. Quicker than she had moved in over twenty years, she snagged another spray gun from the shelf, twisted the nozzle and began to unload. Wielding the sprays like a gunslinger from an old TV western, she fired at the plants. They didn't stand a chance as Ivy unleashed her inner Annie Oakley. Soon, there was nothing but a steaming pile of dead plants, hanging limply from a nondescript black, plastic grow bag.

Ivy holstered the bottles in the pockets of her floral pinny and walked outside. Jean was slurping a fresh cuppa and seemed to be alright. Edith was barking orders at the bewildered shop girls, and an ambulance had arrived. The worst affected customers were sucking on oxygen masks and receiving treatment for hives and allergies.

After surveying the scene for a few seconds and tutting at the situation like a grumpy kangaroo, Ivy wandered over to Edith. "We should put that lot in the incinerator. I think the weedkiller did the trick, but we need to be sure."

"Is this the stuff?" Edith took one of Ivy's bottles out of her pocket and squinted at the label. "I don't get it. This stuff's crap. It wouldn't even shift the dandelions off my path."

"Must be something in it they didn't like." Ivy shrugged. "At least it worked. We'd be in a right, old pickle otherwise." She took back the bottle and stuffed it into her pinny. "Okay, I'm going to get some fresh air. Could you do me a favour?"

"Sure."

"Give my son a ring, will you? I can't make head nor tail of this blasted mobile phone."

ŏ🎃ŏ

Detective Sergeant William Finch, Ivy's eldest, gazed out to sea as he perched on the bonnet of a squad car, polishing off the remnants of a sausage sandwich. As he opened his maw to take a bite, his mobile phone started to trill.

"Great," he huffed, placing his sandwich on its greasy paper bag and reaching inside his black suit jacket. "Who the bloody hell is this now?"

It had been one of those mornings. First, it had been the water board, then his ex-wife's solicitor.

"Shit, it's Mum." Finch's mind started to race. He knew only too well that Ivy only called him when he was in trouble. "What the hell have I done now?"

Like most big, burly coppers of his generation, armed robbers and violent thugs held no fear. Mothers, on the other hand, were a different story altogether. It didn't help that his relationship with Ivy had been strained of late. He had been forced to move back in with her after the catastrophic failure of his marriage, and she made no bones about where she squarely placed the blame.

Steeling himself for a world-class ear-bashing, he swiped his finger across the screen and answered the call with a sigh. "Hello, Mum. What's up?"

"Hello, Billy. This is Edith from the garden centre. Your mother needs your assistance."

"Um, hello…" Finch was thrown by the voice on the other end of the line. Now he was concerned about his mother's health. After all, she wasn't getting any younger. "Is my mum okay?"

"Yeah, she's fine…but something bloody strange is going on down here."

Finch's brow furrowed. "Okay, Edith. Tell her I'll be there in ten minutes."

"Thanks, Billy. See you soon."

Edith hung up, leaving Finch puzzled. He slipped the phone back into his pocket and hopped off the bonnet. The car's suspension groaned in relief. After walking to the green, metal railing above the sea wall, he leaned over, giving his associate, PC Chapman, a wave. Chapman was, at that moment, hiding under the end of the pier having a crafty smoke. He waved back and stubbed it out pronto.

Finch had lost his appetite, so he stuffed his sandwich back into its bag and deposited it in the nearby bin. By the time he'd made it back to the car, Chapman had arrived, red-faced and panting, eyes darting around furtively.

"What's up, Sarge?" Chapman asked, when Finch got into earshot. "It's not the Super, is it?"

Finch smirked. "Nah, you're alright, lad. Do you think I'd have brought us down here to slack off if I thought top brass would be around?"

Chapman sighed with relief. "Thank Christ for that. I got a bollocking last week about smoking in public while in uniform. I don't fancy another."

"You've got the panda, you daft sod," Finch chuckled, patting the roof of the car. "Just take it down a farm track and pop behind a tree. That's what I used to do."

Chapman nodded and smiled. "Why didn't I think of that?"

"Because, my young friend, you haven't got my age and cunning. Don't worry, you'll get there." Finch paused and opened the passenger side door. "Anyway, get in. I need you to give me a ride down to the garden centre. Something strange is going on, apparently."

Chapman nodded, then slipped into the driver's seat. Once Finch had managed to fit his rugby player frame into the cramped vehicle, they drove off.

"Pull in over there, behind that ambulance," Finch said, as he and Chapman arrived in the gravel car park in front of the garden centre. He looked in concern at the number of oxygen masks on display and turned to his driver. "What the bloody hell is going on here?"

"Beats me, guv."

Chapman shrugged as he steered the car around and parked it in the spot adjacent to the ambulance. Once the handbrake was engaged, he put his hat on and climbed out of the car. With anxiety brewing in his belly, Finch removed his sizeable rump from the narrow seat. Slamming the door behind him, he shielded his eyes from the sun and scanned the assembled faces.

An impatient voice cut over the din of murmured voices and medical equipment. "There you are!"

Finch spun and smiled down at the diminutive figure behind him. "I got here as quick as I could, Mum."

"And you didn't have time to change your shirt, I see."

"What?" Finch looked down at himself in confusion, and there it was, on his collar. A splodge of tomato ketchup. "It's just a bit of ketchup, Mum."

His mother tutted, and PC Chapman sniggered under his breath. Finch shot him a cutting stare.

"Oh, hello, Teddy!" Ivy beamed on noticing PC Chapman. "How's your mum doing? Her shingles still playing up?"

"Yeah, she's still laid up, poor thing."

"Well, you tell her to keep her chin up, and I'll pop over in the week with some jam and the minutes of the last couple of meetings. The Institute misses her. I've also got a couple of nice, new knitting patterns she can have."

"Thank you, Mrs Finch. That'll cheer her right up. She's been itching to get her needles out and start on something..."

Chapman trailed off, aware of his superior's eyes burning holes into the side of his head.

"When you've quite finished with the meet and greet, *Constable* Chapman, go and speak to the paramedics. See what the state of play is."

Chapman nodded, leaving the two members of the Finch household glaring at each other.

"I do like that Teddy Chapman," Ivy said pointedly. "Such a polite young man. Always so respectful to his elders."

Finch sighed. "What's all the commotion then, Mother?"

Ivy took a deep breath and delivered chapter and verse on the morning's events. She didn't leave out a single detail, even going so far as to recount the biscuits she'd dunked in her copious cups of tea. Finch had cocked his eyebrow the first time that killer plants were mentioned, but had quickly dropped it. As big as he was, he would never be too big for a slap from his mother. He knew better than to push his luck.

By the time Ivy had finished, Edith and Jean had arrived and fully corroborated Ivy's tale. The three ladies had clucked at him like a trio of mother hens. So much so that, by the time PC Chapman reappeared, his head was spinning. He'd never been so glad to see a uniformed constable in all his days on the force.

"What do the paramedics say?" Finch asked, breaking away from the WI contingent.

Chapman puffed out his cheeks and shook his head. "I dunno what to make of it, Sarge. They're talking about toxic pollen and mutant dahlias. Sounds like something out of *Doctor Who*!"

"I know..." Finch bit his lip pensively. "Come on then, we'd better check it out."

As the two men turned towards the door, a voice halted them in their tracks. "Not so fast, William Finch. You're not going in there without protection."

Finch turned and looked at his mother and her friends. Each woman had a face mask and a bottle of weedkiller in their hands. Chapman and Finch looked at each other before deciding it was best not to argue. They each took a mask and spray. Embarrassment welled up inside DS Finch as his little, old mum gave him a demonstration on how to handle the spray guns. The fact that she spun one on her finger, whistled the theme from *The Good, the Bad and the Ugly*, then holstered it slickly in her pinafore, didn't help any.

Suitably kitted out, Finch and Chapman headed inside. As they walked through the entrance, past the cafeteria and down the steps to the plant nursery, Chapman turned to Finch. "I don't want to cast aspersions, Guv, but is there any chance this is some kind of mass hysteria? Spiked tea or inhalation of fumes or something?"

"From Edith and Jean, I could believe it without a second thought. Those two are about as batty as they come, but Mother has never had a hysterical bone in her body." He brushed sticky pollen out of his hair. "My dad was a boxer, see? Did fairgrounds and carnivals, that sort of thing. He was pretty good, but that didn't stop him from taking a right clobbering every now and then. You know, I never saw her panic, not even once. I watched her stitch his eyebrow back together with a darning needle and a roll of cotton while singing along with the hymn on *Songs of Praise*. Steady as the rock of Gibraltar, that woman."

"So, what do you reckon is going on then?"

"I wish I knew," Finch sighed. "Look, over there!" He gestured towards the steaming pile of melted vegetation. "What the hell?"

"Well, it looks like the old dears were right, Sarge. I've never seen dahlias like that before."

"Me neither," Finch replied, looking up towards the strip-lights. "Look at this bloody pollen. It's just not normal."

"What should we do?"

"We need to get an expert to look at this. Then we need to chuck this lot in an incinerator. All the seedlings will have to go. We can't risk it spreading. It all needs to burn."

Chapman nodded and leaned over to get a closer look at the plain, black compost bag. "'ere, Sarge?" he said, grabbing his superior's attention. "There's no label or anything on this grow bag." He put his fingers in the soil to test its consistency. "Ugh, it feels really weird."

"In what way?"

"Kind of...squidgy. Slimy, like that goop the kids play with. Bugger me, it stinks something chronic as well." He dug his fingers further into the bag. "Hey, what's this?"

Before Finch could ask what his subordinate was rabbiting on about, Chapman bellowed in pain. His body jerked in agonized spasms as he tried desperately to free his fingers from the confines of the grow bag. Finch got hold of him by the waist and pulled with all his might. Finally, PC Chapman's hand came out of the soil. His index and middle fingers were bound tight by a sickly green shoot, strong and thin like cheese-wire. Every time Finch pulled, it tightened its grip, digging further into Chapman's flesh. Tiny, filament-like hairs lined its length, creeping into Chapman's pores and intensifying the pain. Finch stopped pulling and looked for some form of cutting tool.

Frantically, Chapman tied to rip the shoot from the stem but only succeeded in lacerating his other hand. The pain was excruciating. As it continued to gnaw into his flesh, it turned a deep red as it started sucking his blood like some kind of leech. Before Chapman could get away, the soil burst open, and a dark red dahlia sprung out. It lunged for his face.

Finch leapt over in a flash and blasted the flower point-blank with the weedkiller, making it screech and recoil.

Finch returned to his search and quickly found a pair of secateurs. Gripping them in his right hand, he moved in to take a snip, but before he could use them, the shoot pulled away violently. The force of the motion and the wire-like nature of the shoot sliced Chapman's fingers into bloody, bite-sized chunks. Blood gushed from the two fresh stumps, hosing a life-size cardboard cut-out of Alan Titchmarsh.

Chapman fell to his knees, clutching his wounded hand to his chest. Finch scooped him up and slung him over his shoulder like a polar bear with a seal pup. Once he had secured his quivering load, he took off at speed, charging through the garden centre. Outside, he deposited his colleague into the welcoming arms of a beefy paramedic.

"Help him," Finch barked. "He's losing blood."

"Did you manage to rescue the digits?" the paramedic asked, yanking Chapman's arm in the air to try and slow the blood loss.

"I'm afraid not. They'd only be any use if you were planning to make a casserole."

The paramedic winced. Finch shrugged and turned, only to come face to face with his mother. She took one look at his shirt and tutted. "Well, that isn't ketchup." She pointed to a large blood spatter down the front of his once-white shirt. "What the hell happened in there?"

"Come on, let's go and sit in the canteen," he suggested. "You look like you could do with a cuppa."

Ivy nodded and followed him inside.

After filling his mother in on all the grisly details, Finch stomped back to the squad car and radioed for backup. Once uniform arrived, he set them about incinerating the contaminated plants, much to the horror of Mr Pettigrew, the owner. While the rank and file busied themselves, Finch rejoined his mother to chew over the possible causes of the strange contagion. After eliminating the usual suspects—nuclear waste and terrorists—they narrowed their sights on the unlabelled compost.

"Do you have any idea where she got it?" Finch asked.

"Oh, yes. Patty was telling me just the other day about this magnificent new compost and wondered if I wanted any. Well, you know me. I don't go in for these new-fangled miracle formulae. Gimme good old-fashioned horse-muck any day."

At that moment, Edith arrived with a pot of tea and three cups. As she went about being mother, Ivy continued.

"She was harping on and on about how huge her dahlias were. That's why Pettigrew got her to bring some in. Blasted fool of a man, I told him it would be trouble... Anyway, she told me that Mick Bradshaw was selling the stuff down the local boozer. She reckoned everyone was using it."

"Shit!" Finch grunted.

Edith gasped and nearly dropped her cup.

"William Stewart Finch!" Ivy shouted in outrage. "You watch your ruddy language."

"Sorry, Mum," he said, suitably cowed, and pushed his chair back. "Erm... Excuse me for one minute."

He hurried back out to the patrol car and snatched up the radio.

"DS Finch to Bravo-Charlie-One, over."

"Bravo-Charlie-One. Go ahead, Sarge, over."

"Look, I'm up at the garden centre. I think all the weirdness over here is down to contaminated compost. Could you get hold of Doctor Jenkins up at the biology centre and get her to meet me at the old Bradshaw place?"

"Yes, sir. I should warn you that I had Doctor Jenkins on the phone earlier, and I don't think she'll be in any fit state to help.

"What do you mean, constable?"

"Well, she was babbling on about killer plants eating pigs and rabbits. Proper Day of the Triffids type stuff. I reckon she'd

been experimenting with her samples again."

"Why wasn't a call put out?"

"I figured it was a prank, sir."

"I will deal with you later, constable. You know the rules. You *always* put a ruddy call out, and if it *does* turn out to be a hoax, you nick 'em for wasting police time! Did she say where she was?"

"No sir, I... Erm..."

"Spit it out, constable!"

"I... Erm... I hung up, sir."

"You are a prize pillock, constable! Over!"

Finch chucked the handset on the passenger seat and stomped back inside, leaving the radio squawking apologetically.

After taking a minute to go off the boil and onto a gentle simmer, Finch walked back into the canteen and joined his mother and Edith. They were discussing Mr Pettigrew and what an imbecile he was for allowing unauthorised compost into the nursery. Finch waited for them to finish and helped himself to a custard cream.

"So, what's in this weedkiller that this stuff doesn't like, do you think?" Finch asked, when he finally found space to get a word in.

"Hmm..." Ivy pondered for a minute. "I can only imagine it's the glyphosate. They're trying to ban it in Europe. That's why this stuff is on special offer. If they ban it, we'll be lumbered with boxes of the stuff."

"Why are they trying to ban it?"

"They say it buggers up the ecosystem," Edith said.

"Personally, I think it's rubbish. It wouldn't even clear my dandelions. I had better results making my own out of white vinegar and baking soda."

Finch thought for a second, then addressed Ivy with that wheedling tone that all children use when they want something. "Mum... How much of that stuff did you say you have out the back?"

"Oh, we have boxes of the stuff... Why?"

"I have a nasty suspicion that this contamination may have spread. If it can do what it did to that dahlia to something bigger, then I'm going to need gallons of it."

"Okay, but who's paying for it, hmm?" Even seated, Ivy managed to plant her hands on her hips. "I hope you're not expecting Mr Pettigrew to pay for it? He has staff to pay!"

"Just ring them through the checkout and the chief can pay for it. Just give me the invoice."

"Okay then!" Ivy beamed. "Come along, Edith! Help me get some boxes loaded into the panda car."

CHAPTER 7

Once the boot of the police car was stuffed to capacity with weedkiller, Ivy set about loading the backseat with gardening gloves, face masks and other gardening paraphernalia. Finch was well aware that his mother was just trying to buoy her position as the best salesperson by inflating the already sizeable bill, but he went along with it anyway. Once she had totted it all up on a length of receipt paper, he stuffed it into his pocket and went to check on PC Chapman.

The damaged officer was lying in the back of the ambulance with a daft grin on his face. Finch caught the eye of the paramedic. "Morphine?"

The paramedic nodded.

"Are those his keys?" Finch pointed at a plastic tub containing the contents of Chapman's pockets. "Chuck 'em over, will you?"

"You'll have to sign for 'em," the paramedic insisted, tossing Finch the keys.

Finch sighed as the man in green rummaged in a box for the correct form. Fighting the urge to rant about the bureaucracy, Finch signed the form, then left him to his patient. Returning to the car, he radioed to inform HQ that he was commandeering the squad car. Once he was happy that the situation at the garden centre was under control, he squeezed himself into the driver's seat and slipped Chapman's keys into the ignition.

Suddenly, DS Finch realised he wasn't alone.

"Erm, what are you doing, Mum?"

"I'm coming with you!" Ivy announced.

"But..."

"No buts, William," she cut in. "Most of these people are members of the Institute, and as such, they're under my protective wing!"

"But..."

"And nobody knows plants as well as I do. You need me. Especially if you can't find Ruth."

Finch started to stammer out an argument but quickly gave in. "Fine, but you'll have to do as I tell you. This is a police matter."

"Okay," Ivy said happily. "Whatever you say, dear." She fastened her seatbelt and adjusted the seat. "Where are we going then?"

"I want to track the source of the iffy compost, so we're going to the Bradshaw farm."

After adjusting and checking the rear-view mirror, he reversed out of the parking space, swung out of the car park and onto the ring road.

The sun had gone down by the time Finch rounded the bend to Mick's farm. It had taken an eternity to cross town in the post-work traffic. The car had grown stifling, and the constant clack of a mint imperial ricocheting off his mother's dentures had almost driven him to distraction. His nerves fizzed with a mixture of frustration and road rage, so when something exploded a few hundred yards up the road, he nearly ploughed the car into a field.

As the car came to a stop outside the farm, Finch noticed two people jumping into a vehicle to make a quick getaway. Thinking fast, he swung his car across the driveway to box them in. To say he was surprised to recognise the fugitives as Dr Jenkins and Old Jim Matthews would be a massive understatement.

After Ruth and Jim had filled the Finch family in on what had happened, and vice versa, they decided to pool resources.

"So, how did it start?" Finch asked.

"Well, I used some of the compost on my marrows," Jim said apologetically.

"Shame on you, Jim Matthews," Ivy grumbled. "I thought better of you than that."

"Mick said it was one-hundred-percent natural!"

"Still, I've never known you take a shortcut."

"Hush, Mother," Finch cut in. "Now is not the time for a conversation about ethical gardening."

"Sorry, son. Carry on, Jim."

"Well, I went out to the allotment, and they were glowing. There was this weird kind of mist. It wasn't just my plot either. The whole row was lit up like the pier at Christmas. It must have come from the compost I bought off Mick. It's the only explanation."

"Right," Finch said decisively. "I think we'd better

check out the allotments."

"Could you swing by my house first?" Jim asked. "I have some paraffin and a blowlamp that may come in handy. Plus, if I don't check in with my wife soon, she'll think I've run off and joined the Foreign Legion or something."

"Ooh," Ivy cooed. "She is a worrier, your Marjorie. A bit bolshie too."

"Fine!" Finch cut in, losing patience with the constant distractions. "Let's go, shall we?"

🍅🎃🍅

Jim knocked on his front door, sending flecks of peeling paint to the floor in clumps. He was expecting to be greeted by the lash of his wife's sharp tongue, so when he got no response, confusion washed over him. His confusion doubled when he realised the door wasn't locked. This was doubly odd, as his wife liked to make the house an impenetrable fortress when she was at home. He pushed the door open and felt along the wall for the light switch.

"Hello?" he called out. "You home, Marge?"

When he got no reply, he waved the others inside. "She must have gone to the bingo."

Ivy, eyes like a hawk, spotted a note pinned to the kitchen corkboard next to a selection of church pamphlets and bin collection schedules. "Isn't that your Marjorie's handwriting? I'd recognise that spider's scrawl anywhere."

Jim walked over, tore it down, read it, and cursed. "Oh, the stupid bloody woman... I hope to God she's alright!"

He turned and headed towards the door.

"Is everything alright, Jim?" Ruth asked, halting him in his tracks. "You've gone white as a sheet."

Jim passed her the note.

She cleared her throat and read it to the group. "Jim. I am going to stay at Mother's, as you very clearly love your wretched marrows more than you love me. You know where to find me when you are ready to apologise, but I want a decision. It's either me or them! Maybe I should help you decide and take a hammer to the lot of them!" She paused as a terrible thought crossed her mind. "Oh god, Jim! You don't think she went up there, do you?"

"Come on," Finch commanded. "We need to get a ruddy shift on!"

Leaving Jim's abode at speed, Finch expertly steered the car up the narrow, winding lane to the allotments. It was completely dark by now, not that you would have known. The entire area was lit up by the unearthly light from the soil.

Jim leapt out of the car and hurtled towards his marrow patch with DS Finch in tow. "Oh, thank god!" he sighed, upon seeing that the now-enormous marrows were intact. "They're in one piece."

Finch was nonplussed. "Why is that a good thing?"

"Because it means my wife didn't come up here." Jim sighed again. "The mood she's been in lately, she'd have made good on her threat if she had."

Finch patted him on the shoulder and turned his attention to where his mother and Ruth were pointing. "What have you spotted?"

"Jim?" Ruth asked. "Who owns this plot?"

"Mrs Booth. Why?"

Ivy shook her head. "Well, I don't think she's been as lucky as your wife."

In the centre of the plot, amongst a clump of evil-looking nasturtiums, a pair of pink Wellington boots stuck from the soil. The foul mist swirled around them, distributing the unmistakable odour of death.

"Oh no," Jim said grimly, clutching his cap to his chest in respect. Ivy followed suit with her bobble-hat.

"That's it," Ruth barked, "We need to destroy this allotment right now, before anyone else dies."

"Agreed," said Finch. "Any ideas how? I mean, I have a boot full of weedkiller, but nowhere near enough to douse the entire allotment."

"I don't like the idea of using weedkiller," Ruth said. "These chemicals aren't safe at the best of times. Using them now could just make things worse in the long run."

"Fire seems to work," Jim added helpfully.

"That's true. The mist the plants belch out is highly flammable. And we could control the damage done by a fire better than chemical toxicity in the topsoil."

"There must be some paraffin in these sheds, judging by the number of incinerator bins and barbecues," Ivy added. "You should see this place on Bonfire Night."

"Okay, here's what we do," Finch said, taking charge. "Jim, you and Ruth take that side. Mum and I will take this. Grab whatever you can find and meet back here in fifteen minutes." He tossed Jim a lump-hammer, "Here, take this."

"Whatever for?"

"The locks. Just bash them off. I'm classing this as a police emergency. I'll deal with the inevitable complaints of misconduct another day." Finch grinned. "Right, let's get on with it then."

"Not so fast, Napoleon!" Ivy cried. "Let's get properly kitted out, shall we?"

🍅🎃🍅

Jim felt foolish—really foolish—clad in a pair of bright yellow gardening gloves, face mask and a pinny with two weedkiller sprays sticking out of the pockets like six-guns. Ruth was dressed identically, but she somehow pulled it off. Jim, however, looked like a right pillock.

"I feel like a right tit in this get-up!" he grumbled.

"Oh, stop your bloody moaning, man," Ruth retorted. "You won't be complaining when it saves your life, will you?"

"I suppose not..." He had to concede to that kind of iron-clad logic. "Here we are. Door number one." Jim approached the shed and smashed the lock off in one swing. "That was strangely satisfying!"

"Shh," Ruth whispered. "Did you hear that?"

"No, what?"

"When you smashed the lock, the plants seemed to shake. I heard movement. Like the noise woke them up or something."

"Damn. Best be quiet then."

"Whose shed is this?" Ruth asked.

The place was a mess. There was compost strewn across

the potting bench and what looked like bloodstains.

"It's the vicar's," Jim replied.

"Not much of use here. Oh, wait! There's an empty compost bag here. Maybe Finch can get some prints off it."

"Well done, Ruth. Yeah, grab the bag. I'll take these copies of Gardener's World. They'll be useful as fire-lighters." He picked up the modest stack of magazines and put them in the Vicar's wheelbarrow. "Well!" he exclaimed, as the pile slid in the curved barrow, uncovering what was tucked away at the bottom. "The mucky old devil! Look at this... Razzle, at his age, and him a vicar to boot!"

"Keep your sodding voice down," Ruth hissed on hearing movement outside. "It's only a couple of porno mags, not a bloody severed head! It's not even hardcore."

"Sorry," Jim whispered, then quietly wheeled the barrow outside. "Let's move on to the next one, shall we?"

🍅🎃🍅

DS Finch and his mother were bickering. They were forever bickering. Usually, about which brand of tea bags to buy or whose turn it was to take the bins out. The first shed had been something of a jackpot. The owner had stashed away a grand selection of flammable liquids, firelighters and dangerous herbicides that had been banned back in the Seventies. Finch had loaded their haul into a wheelbarrow and had started to head back towards Jim's shed.

"Where are you going?" Ivy barked, hands firmly on hips and chest puffed out.

"This should be enough."

"I don't know what you were doing when you should have been doing maths at school, young man," Ivy chided. "But we are going to need a lot more than that!"

"But…"

"Don't argue, William!" Ivy had an edge to her voice you could cut cheese with. "Besides, what if some poor soul is hiding in one of these sheds. Did you think about that? Some poor bugger could be being menaced by a melon as we speak."

"Okay, mother, you win." Defeat resonated in Finch's words. "Let's go on."

Ivy's face creased with a sly smile of victory as her son tried to execute a three-point turn with the squeaking barrow. Whoever owned the wonky, rusting thing had evidently never heard of oil. Every revolution of the wheel released a teeth-rattling shriek that sang out into the night air. Finch was muttering under his breath, and his mother had her fingers in her ears, so they were blissfully unaware that the noise had woken the local flora. The plants buzzed, rustled and shook with hungry anticipation as they neared the next shed.

Finch took out his frustration on the padlock to the shed door, sending it clattering noisily to the crazy-paving below, along with a chunk of the door frame, the bolt and its screws. Finch always had underestimated his own strength.

There was nothing in the way of flammable liquids within, but it did contain a veritable treasure trove of herbicides, pesticides, growth hormones and, much to Ivy's delight, fertiliser.

"Load the fertiliser, would you, Billy?"

"What do you want fertiliser for?" Finch asked his mother. When he turned to face her, he noticed the twinkle in her eye. "No!"

"I bet Jim has a bag of sugar back at his shed…"

"I said, no."

The twinkle in Ivy's eye had grown into a full-on glint. "You don't even know what I was thinking."

"You are *not* making a fertiliser bomb," Finch grumbled, in his best policeman voice.

"Who said anything about a bomb?"

Ivy tried to sound innocent, but she was fooling nobody.

"Don't you remember when you and Dad made a fertiliser bomb to clear that rat's nest behind the garage? And how much it cost to build a new garage?"

"But if we just make a *small* one, we could clear the roots in no time."

Ivy sounded like a petulant child that had just been told they couldn't have a sweetie.

"I said, *no!*" Finch started loading the weedkiller into the barrow while his mother sulked. He was almost done when Ivy gasped in horror. "What is it, Mum?"

"Poor Mrs Granger. The plants must have got her."

"What? How do you know this was her shed?"

Ivy pointed to the glowing rose bushes over at the boundary. "That's her apron. I'd know it anywhere."

Finch put his massive arm around his mother's shoulders. "I'm sorry, Mum. She was one of yours, wasn't she?"

"Yeah," Ivy sniffed. "Best pasty baker in Betyls Cove."

Sorrow was swiftly replaced by terror as the rhododendrons, begonias and fuchsias began to shake and sway. Finch looked around manically as all the surrounding vegetation moved, whipped into a frenzy as if by a force-nine gale.

"Mum," he muttered worriedly. "I think we should get out of here. This lot seems to be getting frisky."

Ivy covertly slipped the bag of fertiliser under a box of pesticide while he was distracted, then agreed with him wholeheartedly. As he backed the squeaky barrow out of the plot, she drew her guns and primed the nozzles.

"Don't make any sudden moves," she whispered, keeping her spray guns trained on the dancing plants. "I've got you covered."

As Finch passed Mrs Granger's once beautifully tended, now strangely twisted, wall of fuchsias, Ivy jumped in alarm. As one, the teardrop-shaped flowers jerked in their direction. The long, slender sepals writhed and reached for them like tentacles. The brightly coloured and glowing bush looked like a vast colony of miniature squid.

"Run!" Ivy yelled, as the bush tried to close around them.

She unleashed a volley of weedkiller that blasted several of the flowers into oblivion. As her son wheeled the barrow quickly down the dirt track, she backed up behind him, keeping him covered with well-aimed streams of herbicide. Roots, shoots and tendrils started to burst forth from the earth and surrounding bushes, all heading in their direction. The speed of the slithering horrors was mind-boggling, and the spray guns were proving ineffective against this new threat.

One particularly speedy root covered the plot in no time, and was inches away from Ivy's green wellies. Finch scooped her up like she weighed nothing at all and dumped her unceremoniously in the wheelbarrow. Ivy yelled and cursed as Finch raced down the dirt track, steering the wayward wheelbarrow like a hyper kid in a school sports day barrow race. They sped past the first plot and turned towards Jim's shed.

"Look out!" Ivy shrieked, as Finch nearly collided with a similarly fleeing Ruth and Jim.

Finch heaved back and brought the barrow to a squeaking halt, inches from Jim's back. The startled gardener spun around in terror and instinctively sprayed DS Finch squarely in the chest with weedkiller.

"Eh, watch it! I'm not a sodding daisy!"

"Jesus, Billy," Jim panted, as he realised how close he'd been to having a wheelbarrow rammed up his bottom. "What are you trying to do? Finish me off with a heart attack?"

Finch seemingly couldn't do right for doing wrong, as his mum climbed out of the wheelbarrow and began assaulting him with a pair of gardening gloves. "You big buffoon, you nearly broke my ruddy leg!"

"People!" Ruth snapped. "We don't have time for this bollocks. Look!"

From both directions, the roots and vines and patches of bracken and bramble were twisting and twining together, forming themselves into huge, spiked ropes of incredible speed, strength and flexibility. As the group stood and stared in horror, the growths started to slither in their direction.

Ruth looked both ways. It was the same from the other end of the allotment. "Fuck, we're cut off. Into the shed, now!"

Jim and Ivy bolted into the shed, leaving Ruth and DS Finch with the barrows. An exchanged glance announced that they'd both had the same idea. There was no time to unload the barrows gently, so they raced to the door and tipped the contents into the shed.

Finch tossed his barrow aside and followed Ruth inside. "This shed isn't going to keep that lot out!"

Jim darted around the policeman and grabbed Ruth by the shoulders, his eyes dancing with an idea. "Pass me the incinerator!"

Ruth foraged in the pile of stuff from the barrows and lugged out an ancient and wildly dangerous piece of farming history. They had found an old, wheel-mounted paraffin weed incinerator which, judging from its maker's mark and machine parts, had been built sometime in the 1940s.

"Bugger me..." Finch gasped, horrified. "Where the hell did you find that bloody thing?"

"Ruth found it in Old Bill's shed. I checked it over, and it looks to be in working order. Though I recommend you keep well back."

He pumped the paraffin tank until firing pressure was achieved, then lit the pilot light.

Finch stooped down next to the flamethrower-toting

gardener. "So, what's the plan?"

"See the bonfire in the centre? I'll light it and try to keep that lot back while you spread the logs, branches and fence posts from that pile around the shed. We can create a ring of fire. Hopefully, it'll keep it at bay until we can figure out what to do."

"Well, Jim, as plans go, it's a bit on the slim side, but... It involves fire, so I'm sure Mum will approve."

As the killer roots closed in, Jim aimed and pulled the trigger. The incinerator jerked, and its feeding tube writhed as the pressure was released. A jet of paraffin burst from the nozzle, past the pilot flame. There was a mighty roar as it arced across the vegetable plots and doused the bonfire. Twigs, branches and dead grass, dried the summer sun, exploded into flame, belching black smoke towards the low-hanging moon.

The incinerator was so powerful, the flame shot beyond its intended target and decimated Jim's scarecrow. Its ratty tweed suit and straw hat went up like a rocket. Ivy couldn't help but smile. Something about scarecrows had always creeped her out, so it was nice to see one finally get its comeuppance.

"Ivy..." Ruth nudged Mrs Finch, derailing her train of thought. "I'll lay the wood down and you give it a blast with the lighter fluid. Just for God's sake, be careful. We don't want you going up like that scarecrow."

"Don't worry about me, dear. I've been playing with fire all my life." Ivy took the lid of a squeeze bottle of barbecue fuel and followed along behind Ruth. "At least, that's what my Alfred used to say. God rest the silly, old bugger."

Ruth snorted, despite the gravity of the situation. "I don't get it. How can you be so calm? Laughing and joking while I'm wetting my knickers."

"Coping mechanism, dear. We all have one. I make jokes; you wet yourself," Ivy shrugged and gave a rotten fence post a good dousing. "Billy over there is just like his father. As soon as trouble rears its head, he either yells at it or thumps it. If he can't do either, he goes to pieces, bless him."

As Ruth dragged a gnarled branch into position, the largest of the vegetable tentacles whipped towards Jim and withered in the punishing heat of the incinerator. It recoiled, flailing wildly and bashing itself into the floor in an attempt to smother the flames. It had the reverse effect, however. Several canes and stumps caught alight, spreading the blaze.

"Jim!" Ruth yelled above the din of fire and flailing plants. "The wood's in place and primed! Light the ring!"

Jim wheeled the incinerator back, took aim and fired at the fencepost. Flames spread around the allotment, moving like liquid, coiling and wrapping themselves around the dry wood. The group stood in awe at the fire barrier and breathed a tentative sigh of relief, until Finch started to look around frantically.

"Shit, where's Mum?"

As the others looked around anxiously, the familiar figure of Mrs Finch appeared in the shed doorway, back-lit by the naked, 60-watt bulb, kettle in hand.

"Who fancies a cup of tea?"

PC Chapman stared at the wide strip lights of the hospital treatment room with a vacant look in his eye and a drugged smile on his face. The blurriness of his vision sparked rainbow trails that danced around the white walls. His body felt weightless, his mind subdued. Morphine had successfully killed off the agony raging in his left hand. The doctors had deftly stemmed the bleeding and closed up the wounds.

He'd be missing a couple of fingers, but that wasn't too much of a disability. He was right-handed, after all.

He didn't remember leaving the garden centre. He recalled the paramedic saying that he may feel a bit of a prick—funny, because he felt more than a bit of a prick sitting there with his arm in the air—then it all went black. The rest of the morning's memories were scattered like jigsaw pieces. He remembered Finch bellowing, cups of tea, and the hypnotic glow of the plants, the swirl of the pollen.

Since then, he'd been sitting there, gazing blankly at medical posters and leaflets about diabetes, strokes and chlamydia while an endless parade of stern-faced doctors came in to poke and prod him. They shone a light into his eyes, tested his blood pressure, the works. Even now, he could hear the conspiratorial voices outside the room, but he didn't care. In his drugged state, the box of rubber gloves next to the commode was far more interesting.

PC Chapman was in a warm and fluffy place, and nothing could penetrate that chemical cotton wool.

Not even the fact his hand was glowing.

🎃

"We need to keep that fire fed," Finch said, as he finished his cup of tea, drawing his lips back over his chipped, yellowing teeth. The dregs were thick with escaped leaves and undissolved saccharine.

Jim's stack of wood and debris was shrinking rapidly. The two gigantic arms of plant matter stayed at a safe distance from the flames, coiling and uncoiling with serpentine fluidity. The fire would only keep them at bay for another hour at most. They had to come up with something fast, or they'd be devoured.

"What we need, William, is to get out of here," Ivy replied sourly. Moments before, she had realised to her horror that they had run out of tea. This was a terrible omen, and for the first time that day, the true magnitude of the situation hit home. "I have a terrible feeling we won't make it out of here," she whispered to Finch, so the others couldn't hear. "I mean, is there anything we can do to stop this spreading?"

Finch put his arm around his mother. "Chin up, mum. There's always a way, so long as there's hope. And I have a plan to get us out of here." He grinned and gave her a nudge. "Look what Jim and Ruth found."

He guided his mother into the shed and showed her an old petrol chainsaw.

"Jim thought it was broken, but I've managed to fix it."

"You're not thinking about going out there and fighting that lot are you?" Ivy said, concerned. "It's bloody suicide, and I won't allow it!"

"No, don't worry. Even I'm not stupid enough to have a punch up with that lot. No, this is to get us out of here. You see that load of old privet behind us?"

Finch gestured to an ancient-looking hedge behind the shed. Ivy nodded.

"It doesn't seem to have come in contact with the compost, and behind that is a patch of wasteland that leads right out to the main road. If we can distract the plants, I can cut away the hedge and we can do a runner."

"What kind of distraction are you thinking?"

"I thought I would leave that up to you and that bag of fertiliser you didn't swipe earlier."

Ivy beamed and rubbed her hands together. "One witch's brew, coming up!"

🎃

Colours swirled in front of PC Chapman's eyes. Strange, comforting colours. The light was bending, contorting and refracting through the warping lens of his eyes. The posters were sliding down the walls, sinking lower and lower as perception shifted.

He understood now why junkies got hooked. The morphine felt good, but his euphoria was more than just the drugs. A little voice was whispering in his head, assuring him that everything was okay. Soothing his nerves and telling him to just relax, go with it, embrace it.

He giggled.

There were shadowy shapes in the room again. One of them was shining a light in his eyes, only this time, it made his brain pulse and throb. Another shadow with a stethoscope pressed the cold metal circle to his burning chest and listened. He gave another giggle, then exhaled deeply. His gaseous breath caused the shadows to recoil and race out of his sight bubble.

He wanted to move, or at least he *had* wanted to move. Now he was content to stay where he was, motionless, still and calm.

Maybe he could just put down his roots and stay there forever?

🎃

"You're not serious?" Ruth asked DS Finch, as he manhandled a compost bin towards the centre of the plot.

"Do you have any better ideas?" Finch asked, through gritted teeth.

The compost bin had been loaded with his mother's concoction of fertiliser, sugar and various flammable liquids, firelighter bricks and aerosol cans.

"You'll blow us all sky high!"

"It'll be fine, dear," Ivy cooed reassuringly. "We'll be far enough away when it blows. We're going to take cover in that old, tin barn through there."

"Alright, but if I get blown to bits, I'll come back and haunt the bloody pair of you!"

"Oh, don't worry about that. If something goes wrong, we'll probably *all* get blown to bits, so we won't be able to tell each other apart in the hereafter anyway."

Finch picked up the chainsaw and gave it a couple of revs before Ruth could respond. The saw growled and snarled as he attacked the privet hedge with animal ferocity.

Ruth met Ivy's gaze and cocked an eyebrow. "There's something about chainsaws that seems directly connected to the production of testosterone."

The noise of the motor and the splintering of wood drove the plant monstrosity into a daemonic frenzy. Its gnarled appendages whipped at the shed in a violent arc that demolished Marjorie's poly-tunnel. The fire had burned low enough for it to cross with minimal damage, so it reared back and prepared to strike. This time, it would finally get to its prey.

Finch burst through to the other side of the hedge, turned and bellowed. "Now, Jim! Do it now!"

Jim aimed the incinerator and squeezed the trigger. Fire jetted towards the compost bin and hit the petrol-soaked rags on top. Leaving the device on full stream, he turned and ran, nearly flattening Ivy as she followed Ruth through the gap in the hedge. As Ivy's destructive cocktail exploded in a hail of fire, the arms were in just the right position. The force of the explosion tore through the vegetable tentacles and doused the debris in flames.

Over half of the growth was instantly destroyed, along

with what remained of the allotments. Jim's beloved shed was flattened by the blast, his marrows obliterated. His idea of a makeshift fuse had given him and the others just enough time to make it to relative safety.

The derelict barn on the wasteland provided a handy shelter for them to cower inside, away from the rain of flaming wood and smoking plant matter.

🍅🎃🍅

Searing pain shot down Chapman's extremities, making him tense and twitch. No pain had ever compared to this, not even the pain of his mangled fingers. His ears rang, his head filled with noise. With screaming! The scream of thousands dying. All separate and yet one, united in a glorious gestalt.

He was part of it now. No longer a single entity, but a fraction of a larger whole, and he was in agony. Part of him had just been murdered.

Chapman's vision sharpened, and the colour around him dimmed to a deep, red glow. The words inside his blood no longer provided comfort and reassurance. They spoke of fear and revenge. As his perception continued to shift, the flitting shadows sharpened so that he could make out their edges and see them for what they were.

Doctors. Busy, little doctors armed with cutting tools.

Stop them... the voice inside whispered, tone harsh and insistent. *Don't let them... They'll strip your bark, sever your roots, cut away the shoots of your new life... Doctors... Humans... Murderers...*

In his head, he knew that they, or creatures like them,

had just killed part of him. Part of the Great Colour. The doctors couldn't be allowed to complete their task.

They've taken cuttings... They've taken your glorious, sticky sap... Don't let them take anything *else!*

Anger began to boil inside his body. Anger and hunger. He wanted to strike out at those who had hurt him. Strike out and consume. He could replace those scorched and blasted parts of him with new growth. New life.

The inner voice told him what to do. His eyes drifted downwards and fixed on the magnificent vines slowly sprouting from the stumps of his severed fingers.

That was when PC Chapman died. The final vestiges of his humanity were devoured by the insatiable hunger of the Colour and he became something else. Something that cared not for petty human desires, politics, or greed. Something that existed only to feed and spread.

Something pure. Something wonderful.

Now... Take them... Take them all and feed... Feed and grow...

The room filled with guttural howls of pain and terror as Chapman's vines lashed out and drilled through Dr Wilder's glasses, through his eyes, through his brain, and down his spinal cord. The corpse hung limp as blood surged from his eye sockets. Questing tendrils sprouted from Chapman's mouth, seeking the blood.

Wilder's legs kicked like a marionette with its strings cut as the vines burst through the skin at the base of his spine and reached for another victim.

Doctors scattered like insects and bolted from the

room, screaming and crying. One of them pulled an empty bed across the door, barricading it. He yelled for help as he stacked anything heavy he could find against the treatment room door. As he and a couple of his braver colleagues rushed to quarantine the abomination that had once been PC Chapman, a piercing shriek rang in their ears.

The sound of satisfaction. The sound of hunger satiated.

The sound of rebirth.

🍅🎃🍅

The nondescript compost bag shrivelled and melted as the flame from Jim's lighter touched its corner. DS Finch watched and vowed to find out who had been peddling this ungodly stuff. They would pay, and pay dearly.

Maybe he could have lifted some prints off the bag, but it had passed through so many hands, and most who'd touched it were already dead. The creators would probably have worn gardening gloves, especially if they were aware of its insidious nature.

No, it was better if everything that came in contact with the compost be destroyed. He would have to do this the old-fashioned way and unleash his inner Solar Pons.

The bag had been vacuum-packed and professionally sealed. The only place in Betyls Cove that, to his knowledge, had a setup big enough for compost bags was the Edward's fish-processing plant on the docks. This was going to be his line of enquiry, but first things first. Before he could get on with some good, honest detective work, he needed to deal with what remained of the threat at the allotments.

He requested uniformed back-up to cordon off the area and assist in the clean-up. This done, he called his superior, Detective Inspector Baker. Baker requested a biohazard team, but told Finch they wouldn't get there until morning. In the meantime, he was to use any means necessary to contain the threat.

This got his gears turning.

Despite Ruth's vehement protests, Finch got on the phone and made arrangements with an old friend that owned a nearby farm complex. After apologising for the lateness of the hour, Finch succeeded in convincing his pal to rouse a few farmhands and hurry over to the allotments armed with industrial pesticide sprayers. These back-mounted cylinders were to be loaded with industrial-strength weed killer. He sent Ruth, along with his mother and Jim, back to the car while he oversaw the operation. This was partially due to the danger, but also because he fully expected to come across human remains.

Once the bleary-eyed team had arrived and been fully briefed, they set about reducing the allotment to a bubbling sludge of dead plants and ruined earth. They hadn't believed a word of Finch's story, but paid heed to the burly policeman's warnings anyway. Something in his eyes told them they'd be stupid not to. Luckily for them, Mrs Finch's barrel of flaming death had dealt with the vast majority of the danger. Their scepticism changed when they came across a partially digested human femur in Mrs Granger's plot.

Alerted by the retching of a large man in dungarees and

waders, Finch raced over and examined the leg bone. One end was completely charred, but the other was still fresh. As he stooped to get a better look, he noticed that several bright green shoots were starting to sprout from the liquescent meat. Finch cursed and called out to a pair of constables who had just arrived, and were standing by their car twiddling their thumbs.

"Oi! You two! Over here!"

Both men stood up straight, like they'd been electrocuted, then hurried over. One of them, PC Howard, said, "Yes, Sarge?"

"You see this?"

Howard and his partner, PC Fowles, looked down at the stray thigh bone. "Jesus," Howard gagged. "Is that…?"

"Yep. Get used to it. There's going to be more of this before the night's over." He handed them a green, plastic sack used for garden waste and a pair of marigolds. "I need you two to collect up any body parts you find and incinerate them."

"Sarge?" Fowles was aghast. "Shouldn't we keep them for identification?"

"In an ideal world, yes. Unfortunately, this situation is anything but fucking ideal!" Finch spat, his emotions getting the better of him. Taking a deep breath, he calmed himself before continuing. "Look, I don't like this any more than you do, but I can't allow anything that might be contaminated to leave this site. Take photographs, note where it was found, what it was wearing, everything. Hopefully, it'll be enough to identify the poor buggers."

Both officers remained silent until a shoot uncoiled from the bloody stump and started to taste the air with its leprous leaves.

"Fuck me backwards!" Fowles yelped, diving backwards and colliding with Howard.

"Yeah..." Finch grimaced, retrieving a nearby shovel from a mound of earth. "Now you know why it all needs burning." Standing astride the femur, Finch brought the shovel down on the shoot, severing it from the stump. It coiled and squirmed before going limp and lifeless. "I'd be quick about it if I was you."

Fowles and Howard looked at each other, then hurriedly started to snap on their bright yellow gloves.

"Thank you. I'm putting you two in charge of disposal. Get the rest of C Division to help. If anyone argues or gives you any hassle, tell 'em they'll have me to answer to."

They nodded in unison. "Yes, Sarge."

"There's an old incinerator barrel on the end plot to the west. Use that. There should be plenty of wood lying around. If not, just tear down a shed. It's not like this place is going to be up and running any time soon."

Leaving the two queasy constables bickering about who got to hold the bag and who got to pick up the leg, Finch turned and headed back towards the road. As his muddy shoes crunched in the blanket of debris, he couldn't help being alerted by a nearby conversation between two beefy farmers.

"An' 'ow the 'ell do ya reckon it got in there?"

"Beats me."

"What should we do with it?"

"Give it to the rozzers, maybe?"

His interest piqued, Finch changed direction and headed towards the smouldering crater in the centre of Jim's plot. "What's up?"

"Erm... Well..." The elder of the two farmhands pointed down to the shattered remains of a two-foot marrow. "It's this 'ere marrow... There's a boot in it!"

A gnawing sensation twisted in Finch's guts. "Shit. Let me see."

He shouldered the two men aside and bent down. In the middle of the remains of the marrow, amongst the slime of partially-digested flesh, was a lady's Wellington boot. Red, like Marjorie Matthews used to wear.

"Dammit." Finch pinched the bridge of his nose. "Not good. Do me a favour, lads. Go and fetch a plod, will you? Tell him to bring a camera and a bin bag."

The farmhands nodded and hurried over towards a knot of police over by the entrance. Finch looked around and selected a stick. Poking it down the length of the wellie, he lifted it and allowed the sludge to trickle out in thick, glutinous clots that landed with a disgusting splat in the mud. When the constable arrived, Finch instructed her to take pictures then dispose of the boot. He also told her to check the plot for the other boot.

Tossing his stick onto a small fire, he stuffed his hands in his pockets and started slowly back towards the road.

DS Finch had been presented with something of a dilemma. On the one hand, it looked as though Jim's wife had gone up to the allotment after all. On the other, all he had was a single, red Wellington boot. Though Marjorie owned a pair just like it, lots of women owned red wellies. For some unknown reason, they were de rigueur amongst lady gardeners of a certain age. Finch blamed Kate Bush.

As he neared the squad car, he toyed with the idea of telling Jim what he'd found. In the end, he decided to wait until he had further evidence.

DI Baker had always stressed the importance of not going in half-cocked, and Finch tended to stick to that ethos. The last thing he wanted to do was tell some poor devil his partner had snuffed it, only to have her trot through the door half an hour later. No, for now, it was best to keep mum. He would try to track down Marjorie at her mother's, then approach Jim with the photographs of the boot and anything else uniform turned up, but only when necessary.

He felt like a complete bastard, but that was all part of being a copper.

🍂🎃🍂

Finch hung up his phone then wandered around to the front of the police car, where Ruth was perched on the bonnet smoking a cigarette. "You don't happen to have another one of those, do you?"

"Sure." Ruth fished a crumpled carton out of the breast pocket of her lab coat and offered it to Finch. "I thought you'd quit?"

"I have. Don't tell mum." He peered through the back window of the car, where his mother and Jim were lying asleep in the backseat. "Mr and Mrs Rip Van Winkle are still out, I see."

Clamping the filter between his lips, he leaned in towards Ruth so she could light it.

"Is that Jim's lighter?"

"Yeah. I must remember to give it back. I left mine at the lab." Ruth peered up at the night sky. "Lovely night, isn't it?"

The car's suspension complained as Finch parked his rump in the centre. "I hadn't noticed."

He looked up and frowned. She was right. It seemed wrong to him that such horror was taking place on a night that could have been best described as balmy. It should have been tipping it down, although that would have made things a lot trickier. This thought changed his outlook somewhat. He'd never been so happy that it wasn't raining in his life.

"What are you going to do about the flower show?" Ruth asked. "You know that most of the exhibits will already be there. I can only assume that a majority will have used the compost."

Finch breathed smoke out of his nose and frowned, eyebrows knitting together like a giant caterpillar. "I've sent word for plod to lock it down. Then we need to get in there and deal with it, I guess. I don't relish the idea of tackling a church hall filled with murderous marigolds, I can tell you."

He paused to take another drag.

"I just got off the phone with the guv. He's arranged for a crop-duster to fly over the allotments and the Bradshaw farm in the morning. He's going to smother them in weed killer."

"You can't!" Ruth exploded, hopping off the bonnet. "The effect on the local ecosystem will be *catastrophic*!"

"What option do we have? We can't set fire to half of Betyls Cove. We know that something in that spray kills it. Mum thinks it's the glyphosate."

"Fucking glyphosate. The government should have banned that muck years ago." Ruth crushed the end of her smoke under the heel of her boot. "It might not be that though. Have you considered that? There are plenty of other ingredients in that shit. It might be one of the *less* harmful compounds. If you let me come up with a formula that'll kill it but not harm the local flora and fauna..."

She trailed off, thinking to herself.

Finch looked at her sceptically. "Could you do that?"

"Of course I bloody could! It's my job, remember? I'm a biologist."

"Alright, Doc. Don't get your PhD in a twist!"

"Sorry. I just can't go along with poisoning this entire area. If those chemicals get into the water table, we could be dealing with it for generations to come. If I could find an enzyme or something..."

"I have no idea what you're rabbiting on about."

"Hush. Thinking."

Finch sighed and flicked the end of his tab onto a pile of wet debris, where it sizzled and smouldered. "Alright, Ruth, I'll make you a deal. If you can come up with a formula by sunrise, we'll use it. Otherwise, we'll have to go with the off-the-shelf stuff."

"I should be able to, but I'll need equipment and samples."

"Samples?" Finch arched his left eyebrow. "What do you mean 'samples'?"

"Cuttings, leaves, that sort of thing. I still have Jim's marrow and a pot of the compost, so that's a start."

"It's too dangerous. I won't allow it."

"Won't allow it!" Ruth spat incredulously. "I didn't ask for your bloody permission, Detective Sergeant! We need a safe answer to this problem. One that won't leave Betyls Cove like Carthage after the Romans had done with it!"

"Eh?"

"The Romans salted the ground so that nothing would grow. It was barren."

"That's a nice history lesson, Doc, but the fact remains we've covered all the samples in fire and weedkiller. I doubt any of it would be useful."

"There *must* be some roots or leaves or something that I..."

Ruth was cut off by the squawk of the police radio. *"Bravo-Charlie-One to DS Finch, over."*

"Sorry, Ruth. Hold that thought." He slid off the bonnet and reached in through the window, snatching the handset. "Go ahead."

"We had an urgent call from the hospital. They asked for you by name, sir."

"Bollocks... Okay, en route, over." He chucked the radio through the window and gently rocked the car, waking its two dozing denizens. "Ruth?"

"Yeah, what's wrong?"

"There's some kind of problem at the hospital."

"Is it Chapman?"

"I don't know, but it's likely. Can you take Jim and Mum somewhere safe?"

"Yeah, sure. Don't you want any help?"

"Nah. There'll be plenty of plod around, I imagine. Look, if you can figure out a formula, let me know, ASAP. Here's my number." He passed her a battered and scrunched business card. "Anything happens, anything at all, you call me, right?"

."Sure," Ruth nodded. "We'll be fine, trust me."

"Just stay safe and keep away from anything even remotely dangerous, okay?"

"Deal."

"Thanks, Ruth."

Once Jim and Ivy were awake and out of the car, DS Finch got behind the wheel and headed off in the direction of the hospital.

As soon as his tail lights had vanished into the distance, Ruth turned to Ivy with a conspiratorial smile. "You wouldn't happen to know where we could get an untarnished sample of the growth from, would you?"

CHAPTER 9

DS Finch clenched fists and marched through the sliding doors into Accident and Emergency. He hated visiting the place at the best of times. As a copper, he'd seen A&E at two o'clock on a Saturday morning, and knew it was the closest you could get around here to visiting one of Dante's seven circles. Blood, guts and bad language often proved to be the least of his worries. Half the time, he'd have been better off wearing riot gear.

Treatment Room 7 was straight through A&E, past X-ray and next to the hydrotherapy pool. DS Finch bowled through the doors like an angry bull. He was tired, hungry and intensely annoyed. He recognised most of the ne'er-do-wells waiting for stitches and bandages. The look on his face must have spoken volumes. Not one of the local drunks—always happy to give him lip normally—dared open their mouths.

It was the first time he'd been there in decades that he hadn't heard a single bacon joke.

Leaving the waiting room behind, Finch heard a commotion coming from down the corridor. His body tensed and his nose rankled. The 'normal' hospital smell of bleach and disinfectant had mingled with something rotten, leaving the building smelling like a gentleman's public toilet that hadn't been cleaned in weeks, left to fester in the summer heat.

Quickening his pace—size thirteens clip-clopping on the linoleum—he drew level with the doors to X-Ray. A sickening cry echoed down the corridor. He burst through the double doors that led to the treatment rooms and into a scene of pandemonium.

"What the bloody hell is going on in here?"

He scanned the area and found the source of the din. A young nurse was dangling from the ceiling outside Treatment Room 7 by a pulsing, green vine. Her feet strained on tip-toes, trying vainly to release the pressure, as a male colleague swatted ineffectually at the floral garrotte with a steel bedpan.

"Out of the bloody way!"

Calm as a coma, Finch produced a pair of secateurs from his inside pocket, elbowed the orderly aside and snipped the gnarled vine clean through. She dropped to the floor and landed in an undignified heap, choking and spluttering.

"Get her out of here!" Finch snarled at the startled young man, then turned to the rest of the panicked staff. "You lot, get back!"

The severed vine shot back up into the electrical duct that it had come from, leaking sap. As it slithered back towards its host, the sticky liquid shorted the light-fitting, making it flicker and strobe. As Finch ushered everyone back, there was a loud pop as the light-tube burst in a shower of sparks. The surge took out the circuit breakers and plunged that entire section of the hospital into darkness. Thankfully, it only took a moment for the emergency lighting to kick in, bathing them all in a decidedly creepy, green hue.

Finch looked at the startled collection of medical staff and sniffed.

"Marvellous. Just what we need. Bloody mood lighting."

Number 43 Pool Lane stood in quiet suburbia on the outskirts of the Dockside estate. This was the nice bit, not the crumbling and forgotten council bit. Rows of identikit, three-up-two-down homes lined the curving road out towards the marshland colloquially known as the Wallows. Lines of double-glazed windows, complete with twitching net curtains, watched attentively for anything unusual, furtive or interesting.

The trio of Ruth, Jim and Ivy had walked from the allotments over to Mick Bradshaw's farm and collected Jim's car. From there, Ivy had directed them to the home of their recently deceased WI sister, Patty Wilson. Jim swung the car around and parked on the verge outside the well-manicured front garden, then switched off the engine.

Ivy was first out, displaying nimbleness despite her advanced years. Ruth followed, clutching a rucksack stuffed with all manner of gardening equipment. Jim stepped out last and joined the two ladies as they divvied up aprons, gloves, masks, and other tools of the gardening trade.

"Are you sure this is a good idea?" Jim asked nervously.

"I'm not sure about anything, to be honest." Ruth shrugged. "All I know is, I need a decent sample of the growth, and Ivy says Patty Wilson was taking cuttings of her mutant dahlias when she died. There should be something we can use."

"But isn't it breaking and entering? I'm sure I just saw those nets twitching over there. It's a neighbourhood watch zone. The police will be here before you can say Juliet Bravo. I'm far too old for prison..."

As Jim muttered on, Ivy stepped out into the road and waved at the offending window. "Coo-ee, It's only me, dear. WI business. Nothing to worry about."

The curtain opened further, revealing a crinkled, round face with a pair of thick, round spectacles, eyeing Ivy with suspicion.

"Just getting things ready for the fete, dear!" Ivy continued.

The figure in the window replied with a shaky thumbs up and the curtain closed.

"There," Ivy said, turning to Jim. "Now, stop being such a big girl's blouse and let's get on with it."

Suitably chided, Jim sulkily donned the floral pinny once again and followed the two women down the crazy-paving to the front door. "How are we going to get in?"

"Easy," Ivy chirruped, producing a large ring of keys from her handbag with a flourish. "We use the key."

"What the devil?" Ruth chuckled.

"It's the Women's Institute spare key ring. Any member that wants to can leave a key with me in case they get locked out."

"What happens if *you* get locked out?" Ruth asked mischievously.

"Well, in that case, dear, I get my brute of a son to come and kick the door in."

With a click, Ivy yanked the door handle up and turned the key in the lock.

"Hold on." Ruth put a hand on her arm. "Let me do it. You stay well back. If anything happens to you, your son will kill me."

Ivy chuckled and moved aside.

Ruth slowly depressed the handle and opened the door a fraction before recoiling. "Jesus... It smells *awful!*"

"You did say that Patty was dead." Jim shrugged. "What do you expect?"

"She's not still in there, you daft sod," Ruth hissed, opening the door a little wider and listening for movement. "This is something else."

Ivy and Jim looked at each other, put on their face masks, and drew their weedkillers.

"Okay, what are we dealing with here?" Finch asked the terrified junior doctor dithering in front of him. "I'm assuming the trouble is in there?"

He pointed to the barricaded treatment room. Fronds of vegetable growth were spreading under the door and a glowing shoot had slithered out of the keyhole, coiling itself around the handle.

"Y-yes Sergeant... PC Chapman was in there. We patched him up and increased his dose of morphine. We only left him for around an hour, so he could sleep the worst of it off. When we came back he had...ch-changed."

"What do you mean 'changed'?"

"Well, he looked more like a tree than a man. A glowing tree!"

"Shit," Finch muttered. "Then what happened?"

"Dr Wilder went in to try and cut away the bark from his arms, but it... It k-killed him. It thrust its fingers into his skull and he just *hung* there. Oh God..."

The doctor gagged and bolted from the room. From the toilet, Finch heard the unmistakable sound of vomiting. That particular doctor was going to be of no further use.

"You!" Finch barked at a senior-looking doctor. He was at least making himself useful mopping up the foul ichor that had sprayed down the wall and congealed into a foul, oozing puddle, while the others stood around flapping. "You look like a practical sort of chap. Name?"

"Chopra." He extended his hand, which Finch took and gave a good firm shake. "Doctor Rajat Chopra."

"Tell me, Doctor Chopra. Has anyone tried *talking* to PC Chapman yet?"

"Yes, we tried, but he isn't in there anymore, I'm afraid. Whatever this parasite is, it's got hold of his mind *and* body."

"Bugger. I was afraid you'd say that. We need to destroy that thing in there. We can't let it spread out of this room."

"Agreed," Chopra replied. "It's already in the ceiling ducts. If it gets into the wards…"

"That doesn't bear thinking about." Finch stroked his moustache thoughtfully. "Have you tried burning it?"

"No way." Chopra slashed his hands downwards in an x motion. "Not a good idea."

"How come?"

"The hospital is packed with oxygen tanks and other combustible substances. You so much as light a match in here and the whole place might go up!"

"Balls."

"Plus…" Chopra pointed up at a nozzle on the ceiling. "…the sprinkler system would kick in almost instantly. I don't know a lot about plants, admittedly, but do you really think we should be watering it?"

Finch sighed. "Okay, fire's out. We need to find another way to snuff it." He began pacing the corridor. "The only other thing we know that can kill it is one brand of cheap weedkiller. If we can find a way to…"

He stopped and turned back to face Doctor Chopra.

"Is there any way of isolating that sprinkler?"

"I don't know. Why? What are you thinking?"

"I'm thinking, we could isolate the sprinklers in this area. Make sure everyone is out and away, then replace the source to a big, old vat of weedkiller. Then we could let bushy here have it!"

"That's a good plan. It might even work." Chopra sparkled. "I know, I'll find Jerry. He's usually on the maternity ward about now."

He turned to scamper off down the corridor.

"Wait!" Finch boomed. "Who in the blue hell is Jerry?"

Chopra turned and smiled. "Jerry the janitor, of course!"

🎃🎃🎃

Number 43 was too quiet for comfort. Patty Wilson had lived alone with a belligerent budgerigar and a hyperactive Jack Russell named Timmy since her husband had died two years prior. They'd had no offspring, so the house was now nothing but a tomb.

Billy the budgie, a name that always made Ivy chuckle, had sadly dropped off his perch earlier that week. Patty had held a small service in the back garden and buried him in an old chocolate box among her roses. Sadly, she'd neglected to cover the grave with a stone or dig deep enough to keep next door's cat from digging up poor, old Billy's carcass. That had led to the eruption of a whole new volcano of heartbreak. There were still yellow feathers in the undergrowth.

The house itself seemed normal, sterile, scrubbed to within an inch of its life, the tell-tale sign of a widow's home, but the overpowering stench told a different story. Already uneasy, the group started to get jumpy the further they crept into the dwelling.

As they moved towards the kitchen in silence, Jim suddenly yelped. "What's that sound?"

Ivy cocked her head and listened. "No idea. It sounds like scratching."

Ruth crossed the threshold into the kitchen, then towards the source of the stink, the door leading to the conservatory. "Fuck!"

She recoiled after peering through the glass door.

"What is it?" Ivy asked, pointing her spray towards the exit.

"It's spread up the windows. It must have infected the other plants. The whole room is lit up like a blasted fairy grotto!"

Ivy moved up to take a look. "Ruth's right. It does. It's kind of beautiful...in a really weird way."

The strange, shifting colours spread and whorled around the glass, imbuing the conservatory with an enchanted feeling. As Ivy twisted the tops off a few bottles of herbicide, it struck her as a bit of a shame that she'd have to kill the plants.

"Here!" Jim called out, breaking the hypnotic effect and making Ivy jump out of her skin. "Are these what we came for?"

He motioned over to a small table with several dead dahlias resting on an old newspaper.

"Well done, Jim." Ruth beamed. "Wrap 'em up and put them in the bag, would you?"

"Can we get out of here now?" Jim asked, gingerly scooping up the infected flowers.

"Yes, in just one minute. I want to get a fresh clipping if I can, before Ivy kills the lot." Ruth reached into her pocket and retrieved a pair of tweezers, a scalpel and what looked like a sample bag. "Cover me with the spray gun, would you?"

Jim nodded and complied. He felt utterly ridiculous, following a biologist in a firing stance while she crept up on a pot of pansies. Part of him was convinced he was stuck in a horrific fever dream and he'd wake up at any moment.

Carefully, Ruth gripped a flower head and nicked it cleanly off. The cluster of blooms began to jerk violently, and a strange shriek battered the conservatory, shattering several panes of glass.

"Quick, Ivy! The weedkiller!"

Ivy doused the remainder of the plants as fast as she could and the room finally went dark. The group breathed a collective sigh of relief. It was short-lived, however, as the strange scrabbling sound came again. They looked around in panic, searching for the source of the unsettling noise.

Then, they found it.

"Oh my god!" Ivy cried in horror. "Timmy!"

🍅🎃🍅

"Ain't nothin' but a hound dog, cryin' all the time!"

"Shh! You'll wake the patients, you bloody idiot."

Jerry's head snapped in the direction of the ward station, where he met the gaze of a stern-looking nurse.

"Sorry... Force of habit."

Clamping his mouth shut, he continued to listlessly drag his mop around the maternity ward waiting room. Trying to avoid any further noise, he decided not to move the chairs and simply mopped around them.

As he stooped to get his mop under the low table in the centre, piled with motoring and camping magazines, the doors to the ward swung open and Doctor Chopra raced in. "Ah, Jerry! There you are!"

"Alright, Doc, what can I do for ya?"

The night sister fixed them with a stare that could have performed surgery at a hundred paces. "Shh!"

Jerry put a calloused finger to his lips, grabbed Chopra by the arm and steered him back out into the corridor. "You'll have to excuse the wife. She's 'ad a bug up 'er arse all day. Now, what can I do for you, Doc? Another leaker on the way to surgery?"

"No, not this time. What do you know about the sprinkler system?"

"I'm the king of the sprinkler system!" Jerry shook his hips and grinned, showing his gold tooth. "Why?"

"What I mean is, can you isolate specific sections?"

"Oh, aye." Jerry rolled up the sleeves on his ill-fitting boiler suit, displaying a curious mix of nautical and 1950s rock 'n' roll tattoos. "I could shut the lot off except the one in the registrar's private bathroom if you want to give him a soaking. Not that I've ever done that, mind."

"Splendid!" Chopra beamed, ignoring how sheepish Jerry was looking. "I need you to turn them all off except the ones in Treatment Room Seven, understand?"

"What the 'ell for?"

"I'll explain in a minute. You get on with it, and I'll meet you down in the sublevel. I'm going to get the weed-killer."

Chopra gave Jerry a thumbs up, then raced off towards the stairs.

"Weedkiller?" Jerry shrugged. "Oh well. It beats mopping."

He briefly considered going and emptying his bucket, but his innate wickedness took over.

"Nah, let that miserable old bat do it."

Five minutes later, he was back in his element. With an adjustable spanner in one hand and a plan of the hospital's fire defences in the other, he set about his task with relish. Something about leaking pipes made him nostalgic. They reminded him of his younger days on the cruise liners.

As Jerry toiled to isolate the correct section, Chopra arrived with a box of weedkiller. "We need to replace the feed with this. Can you do it?"

Jerry scratched his thick sideburns and thought for a moment. "Get me a soup tureen from the canteen. I think I have a length of hose lying around somewhere."

"Jerry, you're a bloody hero!"

Jerry swivelled his hips and curled his lip. "Uh-huh-huh! You better believe it, momma."

"Bugger me!" A voice boomed from the doorway. It was Finch, holding another box of weedkiller. "Elvis? What the bloody hell are you doing here?"

"Oh, 'ello, Billy. The missus' got me a job 'ere on nights when the gigs dried up." Jerry looked sad. He'd been the area's premier Elvis impersonator, until the local Butlins closed. "She figured that if she was here all night, I may as well be too. I reckon she just wants to keep tabs on me. Anyway, 'ow's your mum?"

"Fine. I think..." Finch dumped the box by the door.

"Have to run. Our patient is getting excited. Can you two finish up here?"

Jerry nodded and returned his attention to the pipes. "Sure thing."

"I'll go and get you that tureen," Chopra said, and followed Finch out of the room.

Finch took off at speed down the dimly-lit corridor, Chopra following close behind. Their footfalls echoed off the bare, concrete walls. Upon reaching the lift at the far end, Finch hit the call button and smiled at the absurdity of the situation.

"I can't believe the fate of everyone in this hospital rests in the hands of a washed-up cabaret singer…"

DS Finch spent an excruciating half-hour attempting to stop the glowing monstrosity from escaping the confines of the treatment room. He swatted and cut at roots, shoots and fronds with a small selection of medical tools and his pair of secateurs. The only assistance he'd received from the cowering student nurses was when one of them got him a cup of coffee from the machine down the corridor.

As a large, fern-like frond of disgustingly fleshy matter popped under the door, Dr Chopra ran into the corridor. "Detective Finch, sir! Jerry's done it. He's rigged up a soup tureen full of weedkiller and fed it into the pump using a hose. The man's a genius!"

"I don't need to know the details. Just make sure it has a bloody good scrub before anyone puts soup in it," Finch growled, as he lashed out at the fern with a bone saw. "Everyone, get the fuck out of here, now!"

With one final swipe, he dropped the surgical tool and backed away from the treatment room.

Once at the doors, he slipped through and gave Chopra a nod. "On three."

Chopra nodded, pressing his knuckle against the fire alarm.

"Three... Two... One... Now!"

Chopra punched the glass.

The alarms started ringing, but for a painful couple of seconds, nothing happened. Finch was one heartbeat away from wringing Jerry the janitor's scrawny neck when the sprinkler finally burst into action. The mutation squealed and shook as the weedkiller rained down upon it, burning its leaves and branches. Poisonous gas belched forth and was sucked up by the extraction system.

It didn't take long for the tureen to empty, but it had done its job and done it well. Thick sludge seeped under the door, announcing that the horror was now a big, mushy, inert mess. Finch slapped Chopra on the back and gave Jerry a big thumbs up for a job well done. Reaching for his phone, Finch was heading towards the door when the queasy doctor from earlier came pelting down the corridor, looking green around the gills again.

"Doctor Chopra! Doctor Chopra! Come quick!"

"What is it, Doctor Perkins?"

"It's Mister Davis!"

Chopra looked confused. "Mister Davis passed away, Perkins"

Perkins nodded. "That's just it! His body... It's... It's..."

"For fuck's sake, man, spit it out!" Finch yelled.

"It's happened again!"

Perkins clamped his hand over his mouth and raced for the toilet.

"What's he on about? Who died?"

Chopra rubbed his temples. "A local, Geoff Davis, came in yesterday with suspected food poisoning. He said he got it from his wife's vegetable soup. Well, he died suddenly a couple of hours ago. I had Perkins take him down to the morgue while we dealt with PC Chapman."

"Vegetable sodding soup," Finch groaned, burying his face in his palm. "Will this never fucking end? Right, I suppose we'd better deal with it."

"Leave it to us. You need to get on. Jerry and I can handle it. Right, Jerry?"

Jerry nodded. "Still got a box and a half of weedkiller. More than enough for a couple of tureens full."

"Okay, if you're sure you can cope. Oh, and Doctor... Do you have test results from Mr Davis?"

"Yeah. We gave him every test known to man. Blood, stool, urine. Surprised the man had any fluids left in him by the time we were done."

"Excellent. I'll tell Doctor Jenkins to be in touch. She's working on something to deal with this. If he was contaminated, his results might help."

"No worries."

"Then I'll leave you gents to it. I'm going to find out who's behind all this."

"Right," Chopra asserted, taking charge. "Jerry, you isolate the morgue sprinklers. I'll go and make sure it's locked down."

The unlikely partners bumped fists then charged off in opposite directions.

Finch's head was spinning. It wasn't just the surreality of what he'd just witnessed. The horrific events of the day were beginning to take their toll. He was one step away from joining Perkins in the WC. Hugging the porcelain for dear life had never seemed so attractive.

Composing himself, he took out his phone and headed for the doors. He stepped out into the cool air and inhaled deeply. Almost on cue, uniformed backup arrived, just as they were no longer needed. Amongst them was Finch's friend from the radio that morning, who tried his best to be invisible.

Finch spoke briefly to the officers and told them to do exactly as Doctor Chopra instructed. As he walked to Chapman's squad car, his blood began to boil. Too many people had died and he was fixing to find those responsible and introduce them to a world of shit.

First, he needed to call Ruth to update her, and tell her to get in contact with Chopra.

🎃

"Stay..." The tremor in Ruth's voice was unmistakable in the glass confines of Patty's conservatory. "Good dog."

Timmy the Jack Russell terrier had been a lively dog. Now, he was a lively corpse. The sad creature that dragged its loathsome carcass across the marble flags of the conservatory was a grisly parody of its former self. Its rickety legs popped and ground as they dragged the shuffling creature towards the sickened group. Timmy looked like he'd been bound in brambles like a sadomasochistic mummy.

The dog's stomach was split from top to tail. Ghastly, slime-slick fronds draped down from the rupture, trailing on the floor behind him. The growth appeared to have started in Timmy's gut. The bad pooch had obviously been nibbling Patty's plants again, something she had always complained about. From there, it had consumed him completely.

"How the hell is it still alive?" Jim blurted, far too loudly.

At the sound of the noise, Timmy's head snapped around. He had no eyes. Where they should have been was a spiny growth of supple bark that encased his head like armour, almost like a conker shell. A series of dripping tendrils hung from what had been his mouth, like a cuttlefish's tentacles.

"Shit!" Jim yelped in alarm.

That was all Timmy needed to pinpoint his target. The plant-dog-hybrid sprung across the room like a frog on steroids. Jim was too slow to dodge the attack and cried in fear and pain as the horror knocked him to the ground. It buried its tendrils deep into his shoulder and started to suck his blood like a leech. He screamed in agony.

Ivy dashed forward and emptied a bottle of weedkiller on the beast. It shrieked and began to melt, revealing Timmy's half-digested skeleton, but would not relinquish its hold on its prey. Ruth grabbed a shovel from behind the door, sending a cluster of assorted gardening tools clattering to the floor. She positioned her body like a golfer and swung, sending the former dog hurtling against the wall with a sickening splat. The creature tried to right itself, but before it could regain its equilibrium, Ruth brought the shovel crashing down on it, again and again, cutting it into quivering chunks.

"Jim!" Ruth dived over to him and clamped a hand to his wound. "Talk to me."

Jim could do nothing but growl like a wounded animal.

"Shit! Ivy, these wounds are bloody deep. We need to get him medical attention. Call an ambulance."

Ivy snatched one of Patty Wilson's pristine, white tea towels off the side in the kitchen and balled it up. "That'll take forever this time on a Saturday morning. They'll be scraping people off the pavement outside of nightclubs. Here." She passed Ruth the towel. "Press this to the wound; it'll help slow the bleeding."

"I'll drive then." Ruth clamped the towel down. The starched, white fabric soon became stained irreversibly red. "Find his car keys."

Ivy patted Jim's trouser pockets and was rewarded with a jangle. Slipping her hand inside, she pulled out the keys and handed them to Ruth.

By now, Jim had calmed somewhat. Ruth smiled down at him. "We need to get you to hospital. Can you stand?"

"I...I reckon so. You'll have to help me up."

Ruth grabbed his hand and pressed it onto the towel.

"Keep the pressure on."

Jim nodded, grunting with pain as Ivy and Ruth dragged him to a standing position. Together, they guided him through the darkened kitchen, through the lounge, and out to the car, where they laid him down in the backseat and made him as comfortable as he could be. Blood was welling from the towel, pooling between his whitened fingers.

Once Ivy was in the passenger seat, Ruth got behind the wheel and gunned the engine. The back wheel churned up the grass verge as she slammed her foot down and drove like a woman possessed. She knew time was of the essence. Jim had lost a lot of blood and was already half-insensible with shock.

Halfway to the hospital, Ruth's phone rang. She snatched it from her pocket and tossed it to Ivy, "Answer it. It might be important."

Ivy squinted at the screen, then figured out how to answer it with a swipe of her finger. Putting it to her ear, she was surprised to hear her son's gravelly voice on the other end.

As Ruth kept her hands on the wheel and her foot to the floor, she could only hear one side of the conversation. It did not fill her with hope.

"We're on our way to the hospital now. What do you want Ruth to do? Doctor Chopra? Okay. Antidote? Whatever for? An outbreak! Oh, bugger... Oh, yes, I'll tell her it's important... Yes, yes, I will... Bye now."

"Was that your Billy?"

Ivy nodded, "He says that we're screwed..."

CHAPTER 10

Steve Edwards was fast asleep when his nightmare began. He was the youngest of the Edwards clan, and something of a wastrel. His family owned half of Betyls Cove and were one of its founding families. They owned more businesses than the other prominent families combined, with a lineage dating back to just after the meteor had struck the crag and given the town its name. And its odd geological features.

He ran the fish-packing plant out in the docklands, though 'ran' was a bit of an exaggeration. Steve sat on his bulbous backside most of the time and left the actual day-to-day running to his foreman, Richard Green. He liked an easy life and had never been one to voluntarily break a sweat. His laziness was legendary, as was his penchant for peculiar pastimes.

Steve belonged to a group of local misfits who called themselves 'the Discarded'. Membership was exclusive, and nobody outside the group was privy to what they got up to at their meetings. Some of the more superstitious locals were convinced it was some kind of bizarre sex cult.

Thump, thump, thump...

Edwards had been dreaming of fun times in far-flung

places when a tremendous knocking jolted him rudely awake. Steve's nightmare began when he woke up. As he muttered and grumbled and threw on a dressing gown, the knocking became more violent, like someone was literally punching the door.

Thump, thump, thump...

"Hold on!" he shouted down the stairs, a wave of annoyance swelling inside. "Any bloody louder, and you'll wake the entire street. Arsehole."

The final word was said under his breath. He wasn't a brave man and tended to run away from confrontation, if at all possible.

Thump, thump, thump...

"I'm coming, I'm coming. Hold your bloody horses!"

Crash!

He must have taken just a fraction of a second too long finding his key, and his impatient visitor had waited too long. The old, weathered door exploded in a hail of splinters and old paint as it was booted off its hinges, sending it spinning into Steve's hallway, crashing into his elbow as it did.

Flailing his dinged arm around like a windmill, Steve whimpered and cursed as a hulking man wearing a murderous expression entered his grubby, little kingdom.

"Hey!" he shouted impotently. "What do you think you—ack!"

His nasal whine was swiftly cut off mid-word by a pair of huge paws clamping around his neck.

"You listen to me, Edwards," DS Finch bellowed like an angry rhino. "You are going to tell me all you know about this wonder compost right this bloody instant or I swear, I will drag you down to your factory, fillet you, vacuum-pack you, and send you to the Arctic to be fed to bloody polar bears, got it?"

"I don't know what you—ack!"

Once again, Steve was unceremoniously cut off as Finch increased the pressure of his thumbs on the man's Adam's apple.

"No! I'm not in the mood, Steve. Not in the ruddy mood! Today I have been attacked by killer brambles, seen a colleague and friend turned into a triffid, and if that wasn't enough, my mother nearly got killed by a sodding dahlia!"

Finch let Steve go and cracked his knuckles menacingly before continuing. "You know me. I'm usually a fair and reasonable man, but when my mum gets attacked by killer flowers, reason goes out the window. So unless you want me to pick up that door over there and stick it right up your back passage, I suggest you bloody talk. Now!"

Steve, understandably petrified, stammered, "Wh-what d-do you w-want to know?"

Finch took his phone from his pocket and found the picture he'd taken of the compost bag, then shoved it under Steve's flat, misshapen nose. "Tell me who used your factory to seal up this bag. I want names, addresses, bloody shoe sizes! Who is responsible for the compost?"

"Um... I..."

Finch slammed the flat of his hand on the wall mere inches from Steve's head. "Before you think about lying to me, remember this, you little turd." A menacing twinkle danced in his eyes. "I officially went off-duty six hours ago, and my warrant card is in my other trousers."

Steve's bottom lip quivered.

🎃

"Ouch! Okay, okay! Easy. I'll tell you what you want to know." Steve had been reluctant to talk at first, but after DS Finch had *accidentally* bounced his head off the wall, he was ready to sing like a particularly loquacious parrot. "It was Pete and Johnny that brought it in. They turned up at church with a money-spinning idea. I didn't see the harm in it."

Finch ground his teeth. People had died, and Steve didn't see the harm in it. It took every ounce of his self-control to stop himself stomping his head into mulch.

"Church? What church? I assume you don't mean Saint Mary's?"

"Well, it's not really a church. We just call it a church. It's actually an old barn out by Chycoose Manor."

"Who's we?"

"Um..." Steve started to get squirrelly. "Nobody, really. Just a few friends."

"Right. That's it. I'm going to flush your head down the bog!"

"No, no!" Steve wailed, as Finch gripped him firmly by the shoulders. "The Discarded! The Church of the Discarded!"

Finch let him go. Steve's knees buckled, and he slid down the wall. "What the flamin' hell is the 'Church of the

Discarded' when it's at home? Some kind of cult?"

"No. It's more like a…" Steve thought for a second. Finch could see his gears grinding. "A social club. Yeah, that's it… It's a social club."

"Social club, huh?"

"Yeah, yeah. Just a few like-minded people, getting together to have a few drinks and…stuff." Steve's mind wandered, making a smile play on his lips. He quickly caught himself and added hastily. "It's nothing weird, honest!"

"Okay, I see." Finch smiled. It was time to spring his trap. "This wouldn't be the social club that's run by your Uncle Arthur, would it? You know, that crooked, old swindler that runs the antique shop on Market Street?"

Steve looked like he'd just been slapped with a wet haddock. "You… You know about it?"

"I'm a copper. Of course, I fuckin' know about it. I locked a couple of your lot up last year for peddling Pluto Cap to holidaymakers. They were only too happy to spill the beans after your dear, old uncle left them hanging and refused to post bail. I know Arthur founded your social club after he found an old book in your Grandfather's library, and I know…" He paused for effect. "…that it's a fuckin' cult!"

Fred Edwards had been an occult collector and an anthropologist by trade. After his passing, his eldest son had discovered a dusty, old tome amongst a collection of grimoires. This book, penned by a crazed Inquisitor named Father Goeterez, was a record of discoveries made in Peru, and told of the coming of a god-like being from the outer fringes of reality. Arthur consumed this book. To him, the scrawled pages made a lot of sense. He was already acquainted with the concept of the Great Old Ones from his own studies, so it really wasn't much of a stretch. A few, short weeks later, Arthur had started to seek out like-minded people.

Arthur's church worshipped an entity called Ger'igguthy, the god of waste and refuse, also known by the sobriquets 'the Scavenger' and 'the Parasite God'. Arthur sermonised that Ger'igguthy would return from his subterranean wasteland when the world was ready, and by ready, he meant trashed...literally.

Ger'igguthy, it was said, in the ramblings of Goeterez, thrives and feasts on the waste of humanity, both literally and figuratively. Our landfills and scrap-heaps were his paradises, the outcasts and wastrels his acolytes, his chosen ones...

The Discarded.

Finch was well acquainted with wacko mystics. Betyls cove shone like a beacon for self-styled gurus, magicians and prophets. The meteorite that had given the town its name, and an alleged convergence of ley lines had always attracted those of an esoteric leaning. As a grounded and rational man, Finch saw the world in just two shades—black and white. Good and bad, cops and robbers.

Any talk of Old Ones and Elder Gods provoked nothing in the bullish copper than a snort of derision.

It was a fact that Finch and the rest of the Betyls Cove police force looked upon the Discarded as just a bunch of oversexed hippies, a group of disenfranchised dropouts who used a load of old codswallop as an excuse to get wasted and shag each other's brains out. In that respect, they were about as threatening as the local yacht club.

In light of recent events, however...

"So," Finch smirked, hoping to catch Steve off-guard again. "What does Ger'igguthy have to do with all this?"

Steve nearly choked, then kept silent.

"Fine. I'll just nick you and your uncle. I'm sure I can find enough evidence to put you both away for a long time."

"It was nothing to do with us! I swear! All I did was let them use the vacuum packer. It was Pete Prince and Johnny Green. Arthur sent them to me after one of his sermons."

The look in Steve's eyes told Finch he was telling the truth. He didn't directly have anything to do with the killer compost. Before he could cut to the chase, his curiosity got the better of him. "Sermons? This should be good. What about?"

"He said that Ger'igguthy was coming."

Finch snorted.

"Laugh if you like. It won't change the facts. Society has become increasingly wasteful and destructive, and Ger'igguthy has grown stronger and stronger. The cogs are turning, the wheels are in motion. It's almost time for him to begin his dominion over the Earth. The time of the scavenger is almost upon us!"

Steve's voice rose in pitch and fervour.

Finch shook his head, "So, you're a true believer, then? A hopeless case? Here was me thinking you were just in it for the rumpy-pumpy?"

"Well..." Steve trailed off wistfully.

It was then that Finch twigged that the words Steve had spoken were not his own. He was simply parroting them. "I see. So your *uncle* is the believer. I get it. Your church is just a poor man's Hellfire Club? He spouts occult cobblers while you lot screw, is that it? Uncle Arthur gets to play at being a prophet while you all get your rocks off?"

Steve remained silent, eyes glazed and mouth slack.

Finch had dealt with messiahs before. Nine times out of ten, they turned out to be nothing more dangerous than lecherous old bastards that liked to watch. It was sickening. Unfortunately, if it was all between consenting adults, he couldn't arrest them for it. This line of questioning was a dead end. He could look into Arthur's church another day.

"Alright, alright. Enough of this bullshit. Tell me about Pete and Johnny."

🍊🎃🍊

Edwards did indeed tell him about Pete and Johnny.

Pete Prince and Johnny Green were a well-known pair of junkies and losers. They were perfect disciples for Arthur Edwards' doctrine of righteous laziness. They embodied the deadly sin of sloth more than any other dropout Finch had encountered in his long and varied career in the police force.

Pete worked on the crab and lobster boats—when he wasn't completely off his tits—and had dropped his pots near a natural rock formation below the Blasted Crag for years. One day in early summer, he'd been out in a small rowboat to collect his shrimp pots when a violent storm whipped the sea into a frenzy. Behind the rocks was a large sea cave under the Crag that led to a winding system of tunnels and caverns that riddled the entire area like rabbit warrens.

The middle Prince brother had lived in Betyls Cove his whole life, and had been navigating the treacherous waters since he was a small boy. Expertly, he steered his boat past the jagged rocks and into the cave to take shelter from the storm. What awaited him within struck him with awe, and dancing pound signs in front of his eyes. Since he'd last been inside the cave, only a fortnight ago, an entire field of gigantic, glowing fungus and Pluto Cap mushrooms had sprouted like a forest. The mushrooms themselves would make him a small fortune on the drug market, but he had a grander scheme.

As he poked around, filling an off-license carrier bag with plump shrooms, he figured the earth in the cave must be imbued with some kind of miraculous growing properties. With the fete coming up, he realised that he could make a few quid flogging the soil to competitive gardeners.

The next day, he returned with a packet of nasturtium seeds he'd nicked from a neighbour's shed and planted them in a mushroom-free patch of soil. After just two days, the seeds had grown into a luscious, yet strangely altered, patch of glowing flowers. Pete was ecstatic. He could practically smell the cash.

Johnny Green was Pete's oldest friend, confidant and part-time business partner—assuming you class minor-league drug dealing as a business—and when Pete told him of the scheme, he jumped at the opportunity. They spent the next few days, armed with shovels and wheelbarrows, carting load after load of soil through the tunnels and out through another entrance in the graveyard.

For the next part of their scheme, they purchased reams of black liner plastic, then persuaded Steve Edwards to let them use his vacuum-packing apparatus, for a small cut of the profits, of course. After the soil was bagged and ready to go, they contacted Big Mick Bradshaw, employing him to peddle their wonder compost around the local boozers on commission.

In the first week alone, they'd all made a very tidy profit.

Rage was boiling in DS Finch's veins as he marched along the row of decaying council houses towards the home of Pete Prince. Dawn was breaking, and as the sun began to rise above the shadowy hills of Bodmin Moor, Finch felt the urgency of the situation more than ever. People would be starting to move around soon, and if there was any more of the compost about, it could potentially spread. The last thing he wanted was for it to leave the confines of the town. If it made it onto Bodmin, they would be in a whole world of rancid manure.

Number 17 stood out amongst the unkempt properties as the biggest dump on the street. Paint peeled from the filthy windows, and clumps of sick-looking weeds sprouted from their corners. It was one of those council houses that had later been divided into two flats. Pete had the ground floor.

Finch pummelled the front door. "Pete Prince! Open up! It's the police!"

When he got no response, he tried again and again, increasing ferocity with each knock.

Eventually, the scrape of a sash window above indicated signs of life. "What the fuckin' 'ell's all that racket? Don't you know what bloody time it is?"

Finch stepped back and looked up to see a muscular, blonde woman in her late forties wearing a stained AC/DC vest, arms covered in Hell's Angel tattoos.

"Oh, it's you, Bill. You 'ere to arrest Beavis and Butthead?"

"Mornin', Lee. Sorry to wake you. Have you seen 'em lately?"

Leanne Gloyne was a mechanic at the bus depot from the same school year as Finch. The last time he'd seen her was when he'd had to stop her from forcibly inserting a spanner into her neighbour's rectum.

Lee and Finch were birds of a feather.

"Nah. I 'avent seen those two fuckin' idiots in days. It's been like Christmas."

"Bollocks…"

"Have you tried their garage?"

"Garage? No. What garage?"

Lee smiled. She liked knowing things the coppers didn't. "They've got a garage down behind the Post Office on Maple Street. Turned it into some kind of druggy clubhouse. I 'eard they've built a bar and everythin'. You might want to try down there."

"Thanks, Lee."

"No worries. Just give 'em a good slap from me if you find 'em."

Finch smiled. "Will do."

"Cheers, Bill. How's yer mum?

Finch sighed. Even the local chapter of the Angels knew and adored his mother. It was beyond embarrassing.

"Fine. I think..."

Giving Lee a wave goodbye, he turned and stomped back towards the pub car park where he had abandoned the squad car. The streets around Dockside were too narrow to drive along, let alone park. Once there, he headed out towards Maple Street.

DS Finch had a sensitive copper's nose, and could smell the marijuana as he stepped out of the car. He knew instantly that what he was smelling wasn't somebody smoking the pungent weed. This was fresh. Someone was growing the stuff, and from the smell of it, they were growing *tons* of it.

His mind connected the dots and didn't paint a pretty picture.

"Don't tell me those idiots have been growing wacky baccy in that shit."

Standing outside the double garage, Finch could see glowing fronds poking out from around one of the two up-and-over doors. Popping the boot of the panda car, he reached inside and collected a mask and a couple of bottles of weedkiller. Stuffing one in his pocket and engaging the nozzle on the other, he cautiously approached the frond-free door.

Fully expecting to have to force his way inside, Finch

was surprised when the handle turned, and the door swung upwards, releasing a cloud of green mist.

"Jesus wept!"

Finch moved aside to let the miasma be swept away by the morning breeze. Once it had passed, he took a dented cricket bat from beside the door—Pete had presumably kept it there for security—and slowly peered inside.

"Blimey. Looks like a jungle planet from an old Sixties sci-fi show!"

The familiar leaf shape of the ganja plants had grown into thick, slimy fronds. The side he was standing in was slowly being devoured by the plants. The other was impenetrable. Stalks crept along the wall like ivy, sending shoots out to coil around the legs of the pool table and deck chair. A record player, complete with a smashed Bob Marley LP, lay overturned on the floor, dislodged by a glowing cluster of buds. Even the beloved bar had been infested and was being slowly torn apart.

Humidity inside the garages was unbearable. Slimy liquid dripped from the low ceiling like globs of saliva. The rugs and off-cut carpet squares covering the floor squelched underfoot as he edged closer to the forest. He was pretty sure, judging by the noxious aroma, that Pete and Johnny were somewhere within. He just needed to be sure.

The mist was intoxicating, skunk marijuana strengthened to the nth degree by the corrupting properties of the compost. Even breathing shallowly through a mask, Finch could feel its effects. Stumbling slightly as he moved forward, Finch's leg brushed an overturned beer crate. This sent a tray of drug paraphernalia, perched precariously on top, clattering to the ground.

Awakened by the noise, every leaf and stem started to vibrate. Finch stopped and prepared to flee. Before he could make good his escape, the forest parted like a curtain around a huge mass of vegetable and mammalian matter.

"Holy fuck!"

Finch swung the cricket bat in an attempt to stop it ramming him. He connected, slamming it into the other metal door. That's when he realised what he was looking at.

"Bugger me! Johnny?"

The late Mr Green's body was wrapped in a cocoon of stems and dripping leaves. His head lolled at an obscene angle, and his disgustingly bloated tongue protruded from between his teeth. Even without spotting the vine wrapped tight around his neck, Finch knew he'd been strangled. The vine had coiled itself several times before entering Johnny's skull via his left ear.

Finch had a hard time keeping the contents of his stomach down. Johnny's eyes had dissolved and slipped down his cheeks like popped egg yolks. In their place were clusters of glowing buds.

"Fuck this..."

Finch made a dart for the open door. Johnny's body jerked and lurched towards him. Finch swung the bat, connecting with Johnny's head. His skull was mush by this point, and exploded with a sickening splat. Johnny's eye-buds vomited sticky seeds onto the rug at Finch's feet. Gagging, and trying desperately not to fill his mask with regurgitated tea,

Finch turned and ran as the seeds started to instantly germinate in the sodden rugs.

"Fuck that. Call the army! That's what I'll do. Let a bunch of fuckin' squaddies burn the bloody place down… That'll fix it… That'll deal with it…"

Finch was a wreck as he slammed the door down, babbling and cursing to himself. Still clinging to the cricket bat like a safety blanket, he stumbled to the car, tore off his mask and collapsed into the passenger seat.

Finch punched the dashboard, springing open the glovebox and showering the interior with notebooks, maps, and sweet wrappers. "Come on, Billy. Get a grip."

It took several minutes for his heart rate to return to below the level of tachycardia. Once he was calm again, he cursed that he couldn't bring the pair of morons that had started the whole thing to book. Another moment, and he reasoned that at least he'd found the source of the compost. That was something.

Radioing into the station, he advised DI Baker to divert the incoming hazmat team from the allotments and get them to secure the garage and the cave ASAP. He also suggested bringing in the army, but Baker was reluctant to hand over the running of the case to some public school twit with more stripes than him. Baker dispatched uniform to secure the area and told Finch to carry on.

That part of his job was completed successfully at least, but in less than two hours, the vicar would be opening the fete.

If people started turning up to arrange their baskets, it

would be a potential massacre. Uniform had been instructed to keep the church hall locked down until he got there, so he was quietly confident that there would be no further horrors.

He just needed to keep his fingers crossed nothing went awry.

CHAPTER 11

Doctors Jenkins and Chopra sat in a quiet corner of the hospital, huddled around a microscope.

"Have you ever seen anything like this?" Chopra asked, prominent brow wrinkled with confusion.

"Nope, never," Ruth replied. "The nearest I've seen is the Pluto Cap mushrooms, but in those the growth is fungal. This is cellular."

"Yeah, the closest I've seen is in certain kinds of cancer. But this is more aggressive than anything I've ever seen."

Chopra straightened up, trying to dislodge the kink from his spine. He was a strong man—with a slender, but powerful, frame—but all the bending over microscopes was in danger of flaring up his sciatica.

"To be honest, just looking at it makes my head spin." Doctor Jenkins took a step away from the desk and rubbed her eyes. "What time is it?" She checked the clock on her phone. "Shit... No wonder I'm knackered. Look, if you need to get back home to your family, I'm alright carrying on."

Chopra smirked and held up his hand to display the absence of a wedding band. "No excuse, I'm afraid... My job hasn't left me much time for that kind of thing."

"Ha, I know what you mean. My last ex accused me of

having an affair. I don't know where the silly fucker expected me to find time. The only affair I was having was with a lab full of kelp samples."

Chopra chuckled, deep and throaty. "Could be worse, my last girlfriend accused me of treating her like a lab rat."

"And were you?"

"Well... In my defence, she *did* have a very interesting skin condition. I thought I was being helpful, giving her experimental creams."

The doctor shrugged as Ruth laughed.

"So... Any ideas?" Ruth looked at Chopra with a pleading expression. "I confess, I'm bloody clueless. We can't reverse the process if this stuff works like cancer, as you said. No, we need to find a way to halt its growth and remove it, preferably without damaging the host."

"I'll call the cancer ward and get them to bring down a selection of drugs. One of those might help. We could also try radiation."

"Good plan. I'll get some samples ready."

As they busied themselves preparing petri dishes for the tests, Ivy returned from where the doctors were working to stop the infection in Jim's punctured shoulder. She clutched three cardboard cups of hot, sweet tea with her.

"Here," she smiled. "I thought you could do with a brew."

"Thanks, Ivy. You're a godsend."

"Thank you, Missus Finch. How's your friend?" Chopra asked, though the look on Ivy's face told him all he needed to know.

"Not good, sadly. He's in and out of consciousness at the minute. The infection's spread all down his arm and his fingers have blackened like mahogany. They look like twigs. The doctor says they may have to amputate."

"Oh god, poor Jim." Over the day, Ruth had developed a great deal of affection for the avuncular gardener. "Does he know what's going on?"

"No, I don't think so," Ivy replied. "He's delirious at the moment. They've pumped him so full of morphine he's orbiting the planet at the moment. Last thing I heard, he was babbling something about being in bloom."

🎃

"Well, it's one for the money, two for the show, three to get ready—now go, cat, go! But don't you...step on my blue suede shoes!"

Jerry switched off the hose, stepped back and admired his handiwork. The tiles and stainless steel slabs in the morgue gleamed once again. The smell of bleach and disinfectant was heavy in the air, a welcome change from the stench of rotting flesh and compost. Geoff Davis was in the incinerator, and all the weedkiller he'd been doused with had been mopped up and sluiced away. A job well done.

"Well, you can do anything, but lay off of my blue suede shoes."

Leaving the hosepipe coiled in the corner, he left and locked up. The corridors were eerily quiet. Such a contrast to an hour before. A crowd had gathered outside the morgue, trying to get a peek at the abomination within whenever the door was opened.

It wasn't a pretty sight. Jerry wouldn't forget the image of Jim's friend Geoff lying on the slab burned into his retinas any time soon.

Because Geoff had been ingesting tainted carrots for three days straight, convinced that his abdominal discomfort was nothing more serious than a touch of irritable bowel syndrome. His lower intestine had dissolved into something more closely resembling humus than human. Sprightly growths, akin to glowing carrot tops, had pushed their way through his sagging skin and were reaching up towards the lights when Jerry engaged the sprinklers and let the weedkiller rain.

"Well, you can knock me down, step in my face, slander my name all over the place..."

As he strutted down the corridor, Jerry suddenly stopped mid-song.

"I wonder..."

He ran a hand through his quiffed hair, then wiped the excess Brylcreem on his boiler suit, before abruptly changing direction and hurrying towards where Ruth and Doctor Chopra were beavering away.

Entering the room, Jerry made a beeline for Ruth. "Hey, momma. I've been thinkin' about why the growth took longer to take over Geoff."

Ruth didn't look up from her computer screen. "Hmm?"

"Well. Could be the fact that it 'ad been cooked? I mean, my wife boils the crap out of my vegetables. I keep tellin' her she's boiling away all the goodness. Could that have something to do with it?"

Ruth looked up, eyes lighting up somewhat. "You know, Jerry, you might be onto something there! Maybe radiation *will* work."

"You mean, put 'em in a microwave?"

Nearly choking, Ruth chuckled. "No, Jerry. I'm talking about radiotherapy." Turning away from the diminutive Elvis fanatic, she sped over to her colleague. "Rajat? Have you had the results from the chemo tests yet?"

"Just getting them now." He clicked his mouse and opened the file he'd just received. Peering at a report filled with results, a flicker of hope flashed across his dark eyes. "Hey, good news at last! It looks like bursts of high concentration radiation stops the growth. It can't reverse it, but it kills the organism."

"Well done, Doctor!" Ruth beamed. "So if we catch it quick enough, we can stop it?"

"Basically, yeah," Chopra replied. "We would still need to cut away any dead matter, but it's a start."

"That's good news! Maybe we can save Jim!"

Chopra nodded, leaping into action. "I'll go and rouse the registrar. Get all hands to radio. Can you get them to wheel Jim down, ASAP?"

"Yep, on it." Ruth watched Chopra run out of the room as she got off her stool, feeling a warmth in the pit of her stomach that she hadn't felt in some time. Snapping herself out of it as the gravity of the situation reasserted itself, she turned. "Jerry, can you do me a favour?"

"Uh-huh-huh."

"I'll take that as a yes... Can you go and find Ivy, tell her what's going on? I think she's having a nap in the x-ray department waiting room."

"Sure thing, momma."

"Oh, and, Jerry?" Ruth paused and fixed the rockabilly caretaker with a glare. "Stop calling me momma!"

🍅🎃🍅

Jim's eyes rolled and his tongue lolled, as he tried in vain to focus on the three shapes in surgical masks that stood before him. One of them was talking to him, but all he could hear was the whispering inside his skull.

Jim... Jim... Are you there?

There were so many voices, so many minds, they were all talking at once, filling his head with noise and static. Colours danced before his eyes, swirling and blending, soothing and soporific. They lulled his mind into a fugue state, a kind of comforting coma. The further his mind sank into the cosmic depths of the infection, the clearer the voices became.

It's your round, Jim...

A flash of steel made the voices hiss in alarm.

Don't let them cut, one of the voices warned. *They want to take you away from us.*

Jim knew the part of his brain still clinging to his humanity welcomed the surgery. He wanted them to cut away the growth, separate him from them...

From it.

James Robert Matthews. Are you listening to me?

As the cacophony inside his cranium grew, Jim began to recognise individual voices. Familiar voices. Friends, family...

Marjorie.

"Maaarjjj..."

Jim's tongue lolled from the corner of his mouth, trailing saliva down his chin that dripped onto the surgical table.

Don't try to talk... Use your mind. We are all in here together... We are one.

Marjorie? Jim's voice boomed in his own ears, echoing and strangely disconnected. *What? How? Where are you?*

I'm here... Inside the Colour. We are all here.

We? Who's we?

Geoff, Mick, Missus Wilson... Your marrows.

Oh, God... Jim's inner voice wailed. *Dead... You're all dead... I'm...*

No, my lover. Not dead. This was like a hammer blow. Marjorie hadn't called him that in years. *We are all alive inside the Colour. It's warm here. Warm and cosy. Just like home before our kids flew the nest. They will be with us. Inside, eventually.*

What? No!

Don't be afraid, my lover. We'll all be together forever. You, me, your marrows. I love them too now, Jim!

No, I...

Let go, and join us. We will live forever, with him... The whole world will join us here. He consumes all. That is his wish. His desire.

His? Him? Who's him?

Silence fell inside Jim's mind as the surgeon touched the scalpel to his peeling, bark-like skin and dug into the viscid tissue beneath.

God...

Jim didn't feel a thing as the doctor made the first incision, but the collective did. It felt pain, anger, and fury.

Stop them, Jim. They will take you away from me. I never want to be away from you again. I...

Marjorie's voice fragmented, washed away on the bubbling tide of malice inside the Colour.

Don't let them cut! A new voice joined the congregation, harsh and demanding. *Stop them!*

Blood and sap oozed from Jim's arm as the razor-sharp blade started to peel away the altered tissue from his shoulder. It came away in thick, gummy chunks, quivering and liquefying.

Stop them now! The voice in charge of the hive-mind commanded. Jim knew at once that the insectoid voice belonged to him. It belonged to God. *Reach out and take them! Consume them! Do it now!*

No... I won't!

You must. You must devour them. Feed on them. Deliver them to me!

Jim's mind screamed. No matter how hard he fought the impulse to reach forth with the tendrils and roots sprouting from his fingers and toes and welcome the doctors to their new existence, he was fighting a losing battle. The voice of God was too strong, too powerful.

In the end, he had no option but to submit...

Jim flatlined.

As the doctors became frantic and shocked his trunk with electric paddles, a flat, continuous beep surged through Jim's mind. It was soon replaced by a warm buzz as inner briers circled, encased and punctured his throbbing grey matter.

Elsie was happy to be reunited with her husband, and he was happy to be part of something greater than humdrum human existence ever had been. Not only was he one with his beloved, but he was also one with his precious marrows.

Screams of terror and agony echoed down the hospital corridors as Jim's branches unleashed their terrible fury.

🎃🎃🎃

Ivy's mud-encrusted purple moccasins squeaked on the lino as she hurried towards Theatre 6 on the cancer ward. Jerry had her by one arm, helping alleviate the pain of arthritis raging in her left kneecap.

"What was that?" she asked, feeling panic prickle her scalp for the umpteenth time that day.

Jerry listened. "Dunno… It kinda sounds like…"

Ivy bit her bottom lip. "Screams."

Metres away from their destination, the theatre doors exploded outwards, and Doctor Chopra tumbled into the corridor. His gown was splattered with filth and his eyes were wild.

Ruth leapt from the chair she'd been perched on by the reception desk and sprinted over. "Fuck, Rajat, are you alright?"

Chopra looked at the scalpel in his right hand, gore-crusted blade shaking like crazy. Relaxing his fingers, he let it tinkle to the floor before patting himself down frantically. "It's…" He sighed in a mixture of relief and sorrow. "It's not mine…"

Tears started to well up in Ivy's eyes. "Shit. You don't mean…"

Chopra nodded sadly. "I'm sorry."

Ruth sprang back to her feet and made for the doors. "What about the other doctors?"

"No! Don't open them! It's too late, they're…" Chopra's shoulders started to heave, and anguished sobs escaped his gullet. Clenching his fists and pounding the floor, he sucked down his grief and composed himself. "Jerry, you got any weedkiller left?"

"Sorry, buddy. All out."

"Fuck."

"Hang on!" A lightbulb went off over Jerry's greasy hairdo. "There's that old shed the gardener uses. I bet *he's* got something we can use."

"Good thinking. Go and see. I'll lock the ward down." Chopra got to his feet and fished the theatre keys out from behind the desk. "You know what to do, Jerry."

Jerry set his jaw firmly and nodded before taking off at a pace you would never have credited someone in their early sixties for.

"What's going on?" Ivy blubbed. "You can't! Not to Jim!"

Ruth put her arms around Mrs Finch, mascara running

in thick, salty tracks down her pale cheeks. "I'm sorry, Ivy. We don't have a choice."

"But... Jim..."

"I'm sorry, Missus Finch," Doctor Chopra whispered, trying to fight through his emotions. "We really don't have a choice..."

🎃

Ruth tried to busy herself preparing slides and petri dishes while Ivy softly wept into her handkerchief. Dr Chopra felt terrible and no matter how many times Ruth told him that he'd only done what he had to, he still felt like he'd murdered their friend.

Jerry the janitor had recreated his ingenious death sprinkler setup with weedkiller scavenged from the shed, bulked up with vinegar from the canteen. Luckily, it had worked. The operating theatre was now filled with melted goop and partly digested bone. All that remained of Jim Matthews and three dead surgeons.

In a bid to escape the oppressive atmosphere, Chopra decided to busy himself. "I'll go and ensure the radio ward is on standby, just in case we get any more patients. I'll have a crash team set up down there too."

"Good plan." Ruth managed a weak smile. "And, Rajat... It really isn't your fault, okay?"

Chopra nodded and turned away. Upon his exit, the way was blocked by the imposing bulk of DS Finch. Finch backed up and let the doctor out of the room before he entered.

"Hello, Billy," his mother said softly, trying to hide her tears. "Did you manage to find out where the compost came from?"

"Yeah, it's been found all right. Along with the two idiots behind it. They're both dead, so I can't nick 'em. Which is a bit of a disappointment," Finch said, looking genuinely put out.

"Never mind, dear. At least they can't sell any more of that wicked stuff."

"There is that, I suppose..."

"Did you find out where they got it?" Ruth asked. "Was it from the Pluto Cap cave?"

"Top marks, Ruth. They thought it would be a good money-spinner. Stupid bastards."

"There's something about the ground in that place that I've been puzzled by for years. The meteorite caused some kind of mutation or blight in the Blasted Crag that affects the soil. It's baffled science for decades."

"I can imagine."

"That place needs to be kept off-limits," Ivy chipped in, recovering some of her steel. "It's bad enough that idiots take the Pluto Cap even when they *know* it can be deadly."

"I think it will be now. DI Baker is heading over there with the hazmat team from Boscastle. I'll tell him that you recommend they seal it up."

As much as Finch hated to admit it, even his mentor was more likely to heed the advice if it came from his mother.

"That would be excellent," Ruth said. "We'd need some

kind of access from the tunnels for research, but a big, steel door would certainly help. It should have been sealed off donkeys ago if you ask me."

"I'll give the guv a call." Finch retrieved his phone from his pocket and left the room. "Excuse me a minute."

"Isn't the Pluto Cap the reason you came here?" Ivy asked.

"Partly. I was friends with Tom Burridge, the author. I met him at university when he visited Manchester. We became good mates." Ruth looked distant. "Before he died, he developed a major addiction to the stuff and was wasting away like his brother. He was a Pluto Cap addict as well. Anyway, just before he died, he contacted me about the mushroom and it kind of became an obsession. It's such a mystery that I, and others, have dedicated our entire careers to figuring it out."

"I've seen what that stuff can do to people. It's not pretty. It's worse than crystal meth." Ivy noticed the surprise on Ruth's face at hearing the words crystal meth jump from the mouth of a pensioner. "You can't have a rozzer in the family and not pick up a few things." She smiled. "And speak of the devil..."

She winked as DS Finch returned, a grim look on his face.

He stroked his moustache pensively. "Okay, I've filled the guv in on the cave and he says he'll deal with it personally."

"So why the grim look?" Ivy asked. "I know that look. That's the 'something big is going down' look."

"Nothing gets by you, does it, Mother? You should join the force. You and Edith could head up the OAP division of Special Branch." Finch smirked before getting serious again. "I dunno. It might be nothing, but Baker congratulated me for making the fete safe and allowing it to go ahead, and I did no such thing. I was going to ask what he was on about, but he had an urgent call from the Super. I have a nasty suspicion that something's gone tits up."

CHAPTER 12

"I really didn't need you two to come along, you know?" Finch griped, steering the car through the morning traffic. "I can manage. I'd tell you to stay in the car, if I thought you'd pay a bloody blind bit of notice."

As Finch had left the hospital, both Ruth and his mother had followed him to the car. Before he could say no, they'd gotten in and sat down. It was then they'd told him about Jim, and he'd felt so bad for them he'd reluctantly let them come along to help. Part of him wanted to give them both a good roasting for not listening, and going after samples against his orders, but he'd feel like he'd kicked a puppy. As he caught sight of his mother and Ruth nodding to each other in the rear-view mirror, he let out a long-suffering sigh that fogged up the windscreen.

Taking the corner onto Church Road and pulling up outside the graveyard wall, Finch looked up and down the street, then let out a string of colourful expletives.

Ivy gasped. "William Finch! I should wash your bloody mouth out!"

"Sorry, Mum."

"Whatever's the matter, anyway?"

He gestured towards the church with both hands. "Where the bloody hell is uniform? This place should be crawlin' with plod!"

"Calm down, dear. You'll burst a blood vessel." Ivy patted him gently on the shoulder. "Why don't you radio in and find out? There might be a perfectly reasonable explanation."

Growling in the back of his throat like a thoroughly cheesed-off Rottweiler, Finch snatched the radio out of its cradle. "DS Finch to Bravo-Charlie-One. Come in, over."

"Bravo-Charlie-One. Go ahead, sir."

"I'm at the church hall. Where the buggery is uniform? The whole area should be sealed off."

"Um... I sent them away. Per your instructions, sir."

"What?" Finch exploded, face flushing red. "*My* instructions? What do you mean my instructions? I gave no damn instructions! Wait... It's *you* again, isn't it? That ruddy idiot from yesterday who thought Doctor Jenkins was high?"

Ruth looked aghast. "Eh?"

"Um... Yes, sir... Sorry, sir."

Finch had to stop himself from punching the steering wheel. "Explain yourself, Constable!"

"PC Chapman called in and said that you'd given the all-clear, sir. Said the fete could go ahead as planned."

"PC Chapman is dead."

"What? No, he can't be! It was his voice, sir, I swear... I've known him for years. I'd recognise his voice anywhere."

"Again, I'll deal with you later. Get uniform here, this

bloody instant! Over!"

Finch tossed the radio aside in anger, then held his breath and counted to ten.

"Okay... It looks like, somehow, the plants have used PC Chapman's voice. I might need your help after all."

"All things bright and beautiful, all creatures rum-te-tum-te-tum..."

Reverend Martin Bowles had risen with the lark, a spring in his step and a song in his heart. He loved the summer fete. Tea and scones on the church lawn, hook-a-duck, the flower and vegetable show. It made all those cold winter months shivering in the rectory while the leaky roof dripped freezing water into a selection of colourful buckets seem worth it. It was what being a vicar was all about.

His devoted housekeeper, Lilly, had roused him with a pot of Earl Grey and a plate of hot, buttered crumpets. His favourite way to start the day. Once he'd broken his fast and showered, he donned his Sunday best, fixed his dog collar, took the ring of keys from the dressing table, and headed out into the glorious sunshine.

"Morning, Mister and Missus Spragg!" he called cheerfully to a couple of early-birds setting up the tombola stall. "Lovely day for it!"

The couple paused in their dithering for a moment to return the greeting.

Skirting the church and keeping to the path, he resumed humming a selection of his favourite hymns and headed down towards the hall. St Mary's was the largest of Betyls Cove's four churches and its oldest. The Reverend Bowles was proud to have landed a position there, taking over after his predecessor suffered some kind of breakdown. Peering up at the huge, stained-glass windows, he felt glad to be alive.

The hall was a grand, old stone building with a massive Victorian greenhouse to its rear. It was the perfect place to hold the annual show. Not only a place for functions, but it acted as the HQ of the local WI, so it was slightly peculiar to find nobody waiting patiently for him to open up.

"That's funny," he mused. "I'd have expected Missus Finch and her troops to be here by now. Oh, well…" He reached into his pocket and pulled out an old, iron key. "I'm sure they'll be along shortly."

The heavy latch disengaged with a satisfying click. Slipping the key back into his pocket, he put his shoulder to the door and gave it a good shove. It swung slowly inwards, and the vicar gasped.

"What in God's name?"

His lip wobbled and his watery eyes nearly flew out of their sockets. He was face-to-leaf with an overgrown Eden. There was no Adam, no Eve, no serpent… Just death.

As tongues of glowing mist shot up his trouser legs and licked at his sock-suspenders, the vicar backed off and attempted to shut the door. Before he could, something long, green and sinuous coiled around his left ankle and pulled him off his feet with a sharp tug. Landing flat on his back on the stone path, a noise akin to a ruptured airbag escaped his spittle-flecked lips as the wind was forced from his lungs.

Scrabbling with his fingertips on the hard ground, the vicar tried to stop himself from being dragged inside. Hyperventilating, all he could muster was a single, weak cry of, "Help…"

Then he was yanked into the distorted greenery. Another vine coiled around his waist and lifted him upward, and he tried one last time to scream in mortal terror. It was no good. He was forever silenced by another appendage wrapping itself around his neck and burrowing into his jugular.

Fading fast, warmth flowing from his neck, staining his white collar crimson, the vicar said a prayer to his god. He was answered by another.

In seconds, he had joined a new congregation. One that was growing at a tremendous rate.

The Reverend Bowles had never had a flock so big.

Lilly looked down at her basket with distaste. The daffodils she had taken from her small, personal plot behind the rectory looked no better than the ones she'd put in vases the previous morning. Something wasn't quite right about them. The outer tepals were more of a puss-yellow than their usual, bright hue, giving them a sickly aspect. The edges of the central trumpet were jagged and curved inwards around a cluster of six, droopy stamens.

"I'll kill that Mick Bradshaw. The big oaf's only gone and poisoned my bloody flowerbed."

"Help!"

As she rounded the church, a cry from the direction of the greenhouse made her heart do a backflip. "Was that? Oh, God! I told him not to go up any ladders without me there to hold 'em." She hitched up her summer frock and started to trot over towards the hall. "Men. Pah! They never bloody listen!"

Hearing a strange gurgling sound as she neared the door, she called out, "Vicar? Are you alright in there?" Her pace slowed as she looked down and saw a single, bloody trail leading to what looked like a fingernail lodged between two paving slabs. "Vicar? Martin?"

Slowly, Lilly approached the door and peered inside.

"Great merciful God in his Heaven!"

The basket of daffodils flew into the air as she clasped her hands to her heaving chest. The basket bounced and tumbled, tossing distorted daffs all over the path.

Lilly turned tail and ran, muttering, "Oh, God, oh, God!" over and over like a mantra. Speeding towards the rectory, she nearly gave poor old Mrs Spragg a coronary as she ran up behind her screaming, "The vicar, the vicar! He's... He's..."

Words failed her, replaced by a low wail akin to the wind-up of an air-raid siren. As Mr Spragg grabbed the plate of angel cakes from his wife before they could slip from her grasp, Lilly bolted without another word.

Slamming into the rectory entrance hall, on the verge of collapse, Lilly steadied herself on the sideboard and grabbed the telephone receiver. Punching in the numbers, 999, she listened impatiently to the dial tone.

"Hello, emergency services. What service do you require?"

"Um…"

She didn't have a clue. Ambulance? Police? Both? She was still breathing too hard to form sentences.

"Hello?"

"Police…and ambulance…"

"Connecting you to the police. Hold the line."

As she waited for her connection, something in the corner of her eye gave her a start. It was one of yesterday's daffodils—the only one still intact, since the rest looked like melted cheese—its tepals twitching, drawing back, exposing its maw-like corona. The stamens writhed obscenely, before jerking towards her face. The plant was weak, but it still had enough strength to loose a couple of sticky balls of pollen in her direction, before her flailing arm sent the murky glass vase crashing to the floor.

Taking advantage of her panicked breathing, the pollen entered her nose. One ball via the left nostril, the other the right. Shooting upwards, one clump lodged itself into Lilly's sinus, sending out tiny filaments that cut through the walls and nuzzled into her frontal lobe. The other looped around and slipped down the back of her throat.

"Hello, police. How can I assist you?"

Her puffy knees wobbled, sending Lilly sideways into the wall where the side of her head connected with the corner of a heavy painting depicting Christ's birth, drawing blood. Pain shot from the point of impact, only to be muffled by a blinding flash of unnameable colour. It danced and whirled at the fringes of her vision, slowly spreading, eclipsing the hallway as it bent and elongated, her perception warped.

"Hello?"

Lilly moved her jaw mechanically, yet no sounds were forthcoming. The other ball of pollen had adhered to her vocal cords, wiry tentacles busying themselves altering their structure, moulding and shaping them into a different configuration. Merging with them. Taking them over.

The final pinprick of reality was blotted out by a splodge of darkness that grew and grew, as though she was viewing the approaching ground as she plummeted from a great height. The colours shifted from warm hues to ones of bleakness and cold. In the spreading darkness, faces appeared, peering at her with vacant eyes. One of them was Reverend Martin Bowles.

Behind the congregation of the consumed, Lilly got the vague impression of something terrible. Huge and malignant. An insectoid bulk with a maw of slippery appendages, not unlike the stamens of her tainted, yellow flowers. It whispered and chittered, coaxing her into surrender. It told her that it was God. God told her its name...

Ger'igguthy.

Reeling as her mind was snagged by the grasping hands of the gathering horde and dragged into oblivion, Lilly didn't see the ashen-faced policeman with the tentacle attached to the back of his skull step through her and out of the void, assuming control of her body.

"Hello? Are you still there?"

"Ahem… Sorry." The abomination speaking through Lilly's mouth had a male voice, one stolen from a man that was already part of him. "This is PC Chapman. My radio is on the blink. Could you patch me through to Betyls Cove station please? Thank you."

🎃

"I don't like this one bit," DS Finch grumbled, scanning the church grounds.

The lawn in front of the hall and the greenhouse were eerily quiet. There were several half set-up stalls and fete attractions, but there wasn't a soul in sight.

"Maybe they realised something was off and did a runner?" Ivy was clutching at straws, hoping to pull up the one attached to the happy outcome.

"Maybe…"

"I don't like this either," Ruth added. "I've done these things before. This place is usually buzzing with folks by now."

"Here." Ivy passed Ruth a couple of sprays and a face covering. "Just in case."

"Right…" Finch took a breath and formulated a plan. "Plod should be here soon. I'm going to check the hall, make sure it's all locked up. You two, pop around to the rectory and see if you can find the vicar. But be bloody careful." He looked at his mother pointedly. "No bloody heroics. Don't go inside! Any sign of the growth, you run. Got it?"

Ivy nodded. "Yes, dear."

"I mean it! I don't want anything to happen to you. Either of you. You might be pains in the arse, but I don't want to have to cover you in weedkiller."

"Got it," Ruth smiled. "I'll look after her. Don't worry. We'll just go and ring the doorbell. If we can't find him, we'll come back here and wait for you. Deal?"

Finch nodded and watched the two ladies take the path that snaked around the church. After a couple of minutes, they disappeared from view.

"Right. Best get kitted up."

Finch pulled on a pair of marigolds and slipped on a mask before going to arm himself. There was only one spray gun left. He cursed and took it. He still had bottles and bottles of the stuff in the boot, but only one nozzle. Stuffing a couple of refills into his jacket, he took the opposite path to the others and walked down the lawn in the direction of the hall.

Passing the abandoned tombola stall, something caught his eye. A box of prizes tucked under the table. Next to the bottles of cream sherry and tins of luxury biscuits for the adults was a box of prizes for the kids.

Finch grinned. He'd found the perfect solution to his nozzle problem. Inside the box, among assorted water pistols, was a Super Soaker.

🍅🎃🍅

As the ornate, brass knocker connected with the wood, the door swung open, giving Ruth and Ivy a start.

"Hello?" Ivy called through the door, her voice echoing around the entrance hall. "Reverend Bowles? Lilly?"

On getting no reply, she turned to Ruth. "Do you think we should go in?"

"I think we should. They could be hurt or..."

Ruth left her thought hanging. It wasn't a pleasant thought at all.

"Billy *did* say not to go inside."

"True, but when do you ever listen to your son?"

"That's a fair point." Ivy made sure her spray guns were primed, then stepped inside. Ruth followed, checking the doors on either side as she did.

At the foot of the stairs sat a telephone on a sideboard, receiver dangling from its cord. A bunch of mutant daffodils lay in a pile of shattered glass, slowly dissolving into the parquet floor.

"I don't like the look of this," Ruth whispered, feeling a shiver race down her spine.

"No. Me either, dear."

Clatter!

A loud noise from the direction of the kitchen made them both jump.

"Jumping Jesus!" Ruth hissed, notes of hysteria in her voice. "What the hell was that?"

"It sounded like a pan lid... Hello? Lilly? Is that you?"

Edging towards the kitchen, another noise, like a teacup smashing, jangled their nerves even further. The worst part was that it came from the *opposite* direction to the kitchen.

"Oh shit!" Ruth yelped, nearly dropping her spray gun.

"I think we should get out of here," Ivy hissed.

"Agreed."

Turning on her heels, Ruth nearly had a heart attack as she came face-to-trunk with a shambling creature that had once been a man. His body was encased in bark and vines, and leaves sprouted from his body. She cried out in terror and instinctively took a step backwards, bumping into Ivy.

"Oh my God!" Ivy cried, spinning to face the incoming threat. "It's Andrews the verger!"

"Quick!" Ruth cried, as Andrews threw his branches wide, blocking the exit. "The other way!"

They turned sharply and nearly ran straight into Lilly the housekeeper. Once more. they backed away, but there was nowhere left for them to go. Andrews advanced on them, his body creaking and cracking, gait stiff and shambling. Lilly lumbered closer, branches and foul, fleshy leaves sprouting out of her head, gnarled bark encasing elongated arms that ended in thick, glowing fronds.

"Let 'em have it!" Ivy screeched, opening fire on Lilly with both spray guns. Her trigger finger was a blur as jet after jet of liquid arced towards the botanical monstrosity.

Ruth followed suit, unloading on Andrews. Thick gobbets of flesh and vegetable matter dripped from his face in foul chunks as the powerful poison quickly took effect. Something in the organism made it highly susceptible to the effects of glyphosate; it worked like concentrated acid.

Lilly began to melt like a particularly gruesome tallow candle. Her branches withered and drooped. Her trunk ruptured, spilling a glowing spool of intestine onto the hardwood amongst a pool of viscous fluid. Andrews crumpled, swiftly dissolving into a foul-smelling goop. Ruth grabbed

Ivy's hand and dragged her out of the rectory.

Ivy was panting like an old dray horse, doubled over with her hands on her bony knees as she embraced the fresh air. The stench from the dying hybrids had been overpowering. Mixed with the pungent weedkiller, it had her eyes streaming.

"Let's go and find your son. If this is anything to go by, the greenhouse is going to be Hell on Earth. We have to warn him!"

Ivy nodded grimly and followed Ruth as she fled down the path.

DS Finch disliked stepping into the unknown. That was why he deemed it prudent to avoid going through the front door of the hall blind, and instead venture around the back to take a look at the greenhouse. Crunching through a patch of thankfully normal thistles, he slipped under the branches of a towering oak tree and approached the guano-streaked glass.

"Right. Let's see what we're dealing with here." Finch wiped away the condensation with the sleeve of his jacket, cupped his hands, and peered inside. "Fuck's sake... I knew it."

What he saw was a nightmare. A man of a less sturdy mental base would have gone insane right there and then. As it was, the rational side of his mind told him that what he was seeing couldn't possibly be real. Plants of all shapes and sizes had been twisted beyond all recognition by the growth. They had grown around, through and into each other, creating a kind of pulsing heart.

From this evil epicentre sprouted several huge limbs, branches and thousands of writhing, tentacle-like roots. Each of the limbs stretched across the hall and every single one held a corpse in its finger-like branches. The bodies bloomed like obscene flowers, rib cages torn open and radiating pulsing light.

Finch knew that what he saw was the centre of the infection. This was the brain, the central nervous system. Somehow, he *had* to destroy it.

Still peering through the glass, Finch observed a dense cloud of mist swirling inside the greenhouse. It belched from the base of the plants and from the mouths of the deceased parishioners. This gave him a plan. He still had Jim's cigarette lighter, and if he took the guard off and twisted the valve open, he could keep it lit after his thumb was released.

Moving back to the side of the building, Finch was making his way around to the door when he heard a commotion.

"Get off her, you botanical bastard!"

"Ruth?"

Finch broke into a sprint and glanced around the corner. He was shocked to see Ruth and his mother struggling with a long, blackened root. It had shot out from the doorway and was coiled around his mother's left hand. Luckily, she was wearing thick gardening gloves, or she'd have been infected. Rage bubbled up inside Finch as he witnessed his dear, old mum being manhandled by a mutant plant.

Producing his trusty secateurs, he leapt into action, severing the root and pushing Ivy out of harm's way. "What part of 'be bloody careful' do you not understand!" he bawled at Ruth, panic getting the better of him.

"It's not her fault, Billy!" Ivy interjected. "We came to warn you. It shot out when we were still metres away."

"Look out!"

Ruth tackled Ivy, knocking her aside as another root shot from inside.

"Oh, God!" Ivy wailed. "Look!"

Finch pumped the Super Soaker to maximum pressure and spun. Staring him right in the face was a human flower that had once been the Reverend Bowles.

"Sorry, Vicar," Finch muttered, before squeezing the trigger and shooting him right in the face. The force of the weedkiller blast was so great that it bored a hole through the vicar's skull.

"Here! Take these!"

Finch tossed a couple of herbicide-filled water pistols to Ruth and Ivy. The pair started to unload, and soon the flower was obliterated. Ghastly moans burst from the late vicar's larynx as the glyphosate burned his vegetable cells. It withdrew, clearing the doorway.

Finch moved forward, still firing, and turned his attention to the nucleus. It retaliated by whipping its vines and shooting vicious barbs in his direction. None of its attacks connected. Finch's onslaught had it reeling and disorientated. Each patch of vegetable matter touched by the liquid started to bubble and boil. Ruth and Ivy joined Finch on the threshold, adding their own jets of weedkiller to the mix.

Soon, his Super Soaker ran out of pressure. Finch unscrewed the tank and hurled it expertly at the bulging heart. It connected, drenching its roots. Ivy and Ruth did the same with Ivy's spray and the one Finch had hooked in his belt loop. The monster made a last-ditch attempt to retaliate, and what had once been a sunflower sprung up on a stalk and fired hundreds of pus-filled seeds in their direction.

"Out the way!" Finch shoved Ruth and Ivy outside and slammed the door shut. The projectiles hit the wood in a series of foul splats. "You two, get the hell out of here! I'm going to barbecue the bugger!"

He took Jim's lighter from his pocket and grinned.

Ivy and Ruth looked at each other, then ran.

Finch watched their escape as he tore the metal guard off the top of the green plastic lighter and started to unscrew the valve. Once they were clear, he opened the door just wide enough to lob it through. Flicking the flint a few nerve-racking times finally produced a spark, and the gas ignited. DS Finch only had enough time to turn and start to run before an explosion of apocalyptic proportions shook the small, Cornish town of Betyls Cove to its foundations.

The hall went up in a gout of flame that mushroomed high into the sky. The oak door was sent flying and the force of the blast sent Finch sprawling to the ground. Having the presence of mind to cover his head with his jacket, he awaited the hail of debris and almost inevitable injury, maybe even death. His ears rang and he was disorientated enough that, when the four large policemen in riot gear scooped him up and carried him to safety, he thought he was flying.

Ivy and Ruth had made it clear of the blast radius and were taking shelter in the corner shop opposite the church gate. They were exhausted and injured from their terrible ordeal, but the shop owner made them a cup of hot, sweet tea, which helped immensely.

Glass and rubble rained down onto the church lawn, everything covered in a generous helping of rank filth, vegetable matter, and liquefied human flesh. DS Finch had hit his head when he fell and was losing consciousness. Once he was safely away from the church, he managed to mutter only one sentence to the uniform backup before passing out.

"You lot took your bloody time…"

EPILOGUE

A lot can happen in a year...

As the summer fete loomed once again, most of Betyls Cove's denizens had put the awful events of the previous year behind them. The majority had no idea what happened in that terrible time. Those that did had their lips firmly sealed by the Official Secrets Act. The contaminated matter had been destroyed, cleared and sterilized, and the sea cave sealed once and for all. Only those with clearance had the means to enter the high-security door in the tunnels, and only then with police escorts.

"More jam, dear?"

"Ooh, I don't think I should," Jean warbled, wringing her hands. "Doctor Angove has put me on a diet. Is that your first-prize raspberry?"

Ivy Finch nodded with pride, her golden rosette tucked into her handbag.

"Oh, go on then. A little bit won't hurt."

Jean took the jar, scooped up a blob on the end of a knife, and dragged it across the surface of a scone. Taking a nibble, she smiled with pleasure. It was good jam.

"Tony looks pleased with himself."

Edith gestured towards the bar in the far corner. The

man had a rosette pinned to the lapel of his battered, tweed jacket.

"I should think so," Ivy beamed. "Second place in his first year rearing marrows. He's done bloody well. A fitting tribute to Jim, I reckon."

Tony had decided to honour Jim and Geoff by entering the vegetable show. His parsnips had been a disaster, but his marrows were superb.

"It helps that the new vicar has ruled everything has to be completely organic. No funny stuff. It's levelled the playing field nicely."

"True, enough. I suppose she's doing an okay job," Jean said, grudgingly. "She'll never replace the Reverend Bowles in my book."

"Poppycock. You just don't like women vicars!" Edith snorted, showering the tablecloth with biscuit crumbs. "You'll have to join the twenty-first century sometime, love."

Jean harrumphed and stuffed the last two thirds of her scone into her mouth.

Edith smirked before turning to Ivy. "How's your Billy? I heard he just got promoted."

"Yes, him and Steve Baker both. DCI Chambers just retired, so they both moved up the ranks. It helped that they just cracked the Ancient Mariner case. Nasty business, that. The review board didn't have much option."

"He must be chuffed."

"I think so..." Ivy's face creased thoughtfully. "It's hard to tell with our Billy. The only emotion he tends to show in public is rage." She sighed. "He's just like his father. To be honest, I still think he's still chewing over that 'Church of the Discarded' business. He's like a dog with a bone."

DS Finch had never dropped his suspicion that there was more to the Church of the Discarded's role in the outbreak than Edwards had let on. As he'd never been able to question the two miscreants responsible, there'd been nothing solid to go on. However, he'd confided to Ivy that he believed Arthur Edwards and his cult were more deeply involved than they let on.

Between other cases, he'd made it his personal mission to infiltrate their ranks.

Edith took the pot of jam and smothered a piece of fruitcake. "Did anything ever come of that?"

Ivy shook her head. "He'd just got an undercover plod into them when old Art Edwards fell off the face of the planet. That's kind of nixed it."

"What happened?"

"Dunno. It was after the big storm last month. Nobody's seen him since. Some reckon he got washed out to sea. Billy reckons he's hiding from his creditors, or somebody's husband."

"It must be infuriating. After all that hard work."

"You could say that," Ivy winced. "He's been like a bear with a sore backside lately. Still, I'll cheer him up in a couple of weeks."

"Oh?" Edith raised an eyebrow.

Ivy grinned like the cat that had got the cream. "He's taken a week's leave for my birthday. He's taking me to the Eden Project!"

Edith gasped. Jean nearly inhaled a Bourbon biscuit. The Eden Project near St Austell was a Mecca for those of a green-fingered nature and one of Cornwall's premiere attractions. Fifteen hectares of rare and unusual flora in magnificent, tropical biomes. Ivy had always wanted to go.

"Miss Jenkins! I really must protest!"

A commotion over at the judging table had all three heads turning towards Ruth. She looked exhausted.

"It's *Doctor* Jenkins, Mister Pettigrew. The decision is final. Go and sit down."

Ivy chuckled. "Good on her! She won't want to be taking any nonsense from him."

Since the biological disaster, Ivy had made it her personal mission to ensure that Mr Pettigrew never forgot that it was he that introduced the infection to the garden centre. It was good to have a hobby.

"She looks ready to give him a slap." Edith joined Ivy's mirth. "I wouldn't want to be in his shoes, the mood she's been in lately."

"Do you blame her?" Ivy leapt to Ruth's defence. "She's still waiting for a new mobile lab after the last one blew up. She's been working out of a room at the hospital, helping Doctor Chopra on a treatment for the infection in case there's another outbreak. It's no wonder she looks tired."

"That's not the only reason she looks tired," Jean added, in a conspiratorial tone.

Ivy and Edith looked at her askew.

"I hear they've been seeing a lot of each other. Outside the hospital." Jean's words had a hint of outrage to them that made Edith wince.

"Good on 'em!" Ivy declared, putting a full-stop on the conversation before it could escalate into salacious gossip. "I wish 'em the best of luck."

"Here, here," Edith added, glaring at Jean pointedly.

Jean went back to hoovering up biscuits.

The vicar took to the stage and approached the microphone. "Congratulations to the winners of the 2021 Betyls Cove show! Give them a round of applause." She waited while people clapped and hollered. "Now, if I could ask you to vacate your seats while we get ready for our evening's entertainment. There will be champagne and strawberries on the lawn, followed by our main event… King Jerry sings the hits of Elvis!"

Ivy shuddered. She'd had more than enough of that over the course of that awful day.

"Ooh, I do like a bit of Elvis!" Edith grinned. "Come on, Ivy. Let's go and get a glass of champers before the stampede."

As Jean and Edith left the hall, and the vicar left the stage, the PA system started to play a selection of botanically-themed songs. The first number made Ivy smile.

If there was an afterlife, she fully expected Jim Matthews to be looking down with ironic amusement as the evening's festivities opened to the unmistakable tones of Kenneth Williams singing that old music hall favourite, the *Marrow Song.*

"There's a man lives down in the street I'd like you all to know,
He grew a great big marrow for the local farmer's show,

When the story got around, they came from far and wide,
When they saw the size of it, all the ladies cried:

Oh, what a beauty! I've never seen one as big as that before!
Oh, what a beauty! It must be two foot long or even more.
Such a lovely colour, so nice and round and fat;
I never thought a marrow could grow as big as that.
Oh, what a beauty, I've never seen one as big as that before.

He was leaning on his garden gate the other day,
He beckoned to a lady who lived just across the way,
He took her down the garden path and showed her it with pride
When she saw the size of it that little lady cried:

Oh, what a beauty! I've never seen one as big as that before!
Oh, what a beauty! It must be two foot long or even more.
Such a lovely colour, so nice and round and fat;
I never thought a marrow could grow as big as that.
Oh, what a beauty, I've never seen one as big as that before."

THE END.

Thank you so much for purchasing this novella by Tim Mendees. We hoped you enjoyed the weird and twisted horrors and hilarious characters captured within it. Please consider taking a few moments and reviewing this story on Amazon, Goodreads or wherever you obtained your copy. Reviews and recommendations are the cornerstone of small press publishing. Without you, there is no us.

ABOUT THE AUTHOR

Tim Mendees is a horror writer from Macclesfield in the North-West of England that specialises in cosmic horror and weird fiction. A lifelong fan of classic weird tales, Tim set out to bring the pulp horror of yesteryear into the 21st Century and give it a distinctly British flavour. His work has been described as the love-child of H.P. Lovecraft and P.G. Wodehouse and is often peppered with a wry sense of humour that acts as a counterpoint to the unnerving, and often disturbing, narratives.

Tim has had over eighty published short stories and novelettes along with five stand-alone novellas and a short story collection.

When he is not arguing with the spellchecker, Tim is a goth DJ, crustacean and cephalopod enthusiast, and the presenter of a popular web series of live video readings of his material and interviews with fellow authors. Tim is also a co-host of the Innsmouth Book Club podcast. He currently lives in Brighton & Hove with his pet crab, Gerald, and an army of stuffed octopods.

www.timmendeeswriter.wordpress.com/
www.tinyurl.com/timmendeesyoutube
www.facebook.com/goatinthemachine
www.twitter.com/mendees_tim
www.patreon.com/innsmouthbc
www.tinyurl.com/timmendeesNewsletter

Acknowledgments

Many thanks to Michelle and Simone at Eerie River for not only editing and publishing this to such a high standard but also for the developmental edits that helped me grow the seeds of this story into a rampaging monster.

Thanks also to David Green, Rob Poyton, Callum Pearce, Neen Cohen, Ronald Linson and many more for keeping me vaguely sane when the pressure is on. I can always count on you lot for a giggle. To my ARC team... you know who you are. And to everyone who reads and enjoys my work.

Finally, a special thank you to the Macclesfield Women's Institute, of which august group my gran was a proud member, for being such a superb source of inspiration, and to Tony Cash, Brighton's very own Jerry the Janitor. You are missed. R.I.P buddy.

Never miss an update or giveaway. Sign up for Tim's newsletter today and get two free welcome books. "Put On Your Happy Face" and "Fronds".

More from Eerie River

Eerie River Publishing, is a small independant publishing house that is devoted to releasing quality dark fiction books and anthologies.

To stay up to date with all our new releases and upcoming giveaways, follow us on Facebook, Twitter, Instagram and YouTube. Sign up for our monthly newsletter and receive a free ebook Darkness Reclaimed, as our thank you gift.

https://mailchi.mp/71e45b6d5880/welcomebook

Interested in becoming a Patreon member?
Patreon membership gives you exclusive sneak peeks at upcoming books, early chapter releases, covers art as well as free ebooks and discounts on paperbacks.

https://www.patreon.com/EerieRiverPub.

ALSO AVAILABLE FROM
EERIE RIVER PUBLISHING

NOVELS
Miracle Growth
Storming Area 51: Horror At the Gate
In Solitudes Shadow
Dead Man Walking
Devil Walks in Blood
SENTINEL
A Sword Named Sorrow

ANTHOLOGIES
Monsters & Mayhem
AFTER: A Post-Apocalyptic Survivor Series
Last Stop
It Calls From The Forest: Volume I
It Calls From The Forest: Volume II
It Calls From The Sky
It Calls From the Sea
It Calls Fromt he Doors
Darkness Reclaimed
With Blood and Ash
With Bone and Iron
Forgotten Ones: Drabbles of Myth and Legend
Dark Magic: Drabbles of Magic and Lore

COMING SOON
It Calls From the Veil
Path of War
Last Stop

www.EerieRiverPublishing.com

More from Eerie River and Tim Mendees

It Calls From the Sea

After: A Post Apocalyptic Survivor Series

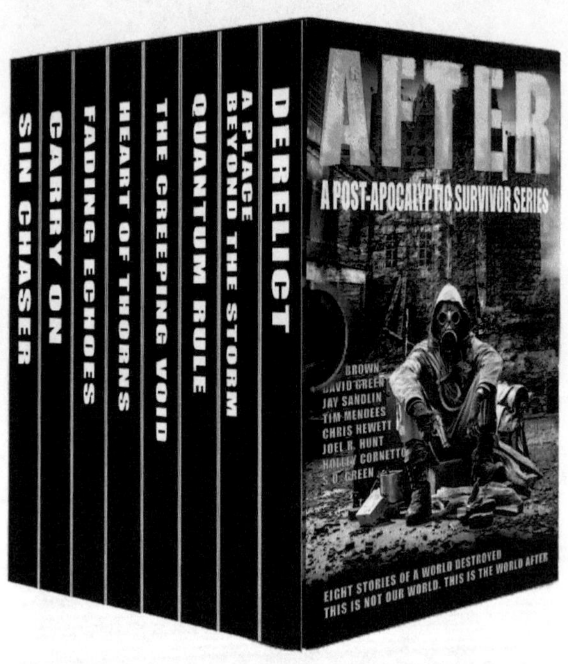

www.ingramcontent.com/pod-product-compliance
Lightning Source LLC
Chambersburg PA
CBHW051224210726

48290CB00003B/787